Dear

continue to ⬭ ⬭ ⬭ ⬭ NG.

Ineffk

Dec. '89

GOODBYE, CARLETON HIGH

B.J. Bond

Cover by Laurie McGaw

Scholastic-TAB Publications Ltd.,
123 Newkirk Road, Richmond Hill, Ontario, Canada

Canadian Cataloguing in Publication Data

Bond, B. J.
    Goodbye, Carleton High

ISBN 0-590-71124-5

I. Title.

PS8553.052G66   C813'.54   C82-095350-4
PR9199.3.B66G66

1st printing 1983   **Printed in Canada**

The author acknowledges use of the following passages:

"Naming of Parts" by Henry Reed from *A Map of Verona* © 1946. Reprinted by permission of Jonathan Cape, London.

Page 129 from "Ode to a Nightingale" by John Keats.

I am graetly indetted to my freind, Cathy Robinson, who tiped the manuskprit from my untidee and missplled notes, and withuot whos hlep this booke wood never hav ben writeen.

Albert ("Falko") Falkenheimer

1.

They say anything that can go wrong *will* go wrong, and maybe it's true. Three months ago I thought things could only get worse. I was flunking most of my courses, Cathy was acting kind of aloof, my parents were ready to kill me, and the principal was just looking for the right chance to suspend me.

Outside it was spring. Through the chinks in the blinds I could see sunshine, butter-candy yellow, and a warm breeze was tossing the new pink blossoms of the hawthorn trees in the school-yard. But inside, in Mr. Harrad's English class, it was still winter. Deadly blasts of icy air were being pumped out of Old Harrad's desk, where he kept his refrigeration machine. I couldn't see it but I knew it was there. And it was pointed right at the back of the classroom, where I sat. Goose-bumps appeared on my arms and I hunched further forward over my desk.

All week we'd been studying parts of speech. I'd memorized some lines of a Henry Reed poem because it reminded me of school:

Today we have naming of parts. Yesterday,
We had daily cleaning. And tomorrow
morning,
We shall have what to do after firing. But
today,
Today we have naming of parts. Japonica
Glistens like coral in all the neighbouring
gardens,
　　　And today we have naming of parts.

Harrad really loved doing parts of speech. He'd
hurl verbs from the front of the room and we'd
watch them scatter in cold confusion. Nouns
would mince down the aisles in icy array and
poor overworked adjectives and adverbs would
shuffle along aimlessly, stamping their feet
against the bitter blast of Harrad's refrigeration
machine. Finally they'd all end up in a heap at
the back of the room and scramble over one another, looking for a warm corner before arranging
themselves dutifully into an English sentence.

It was impossible to hide in Harrad's class even
when the blinds were drawn and the room was
hidden in darkness broken only by the 300-watt
light from Harrad's overhead projector; impossible to hide even when you scrunched yourself
down real small over your desk. With Mrs. Cost,
who taught Math, I could often make myself in-
visible—especially when she used her overhead
projector—but it never worked on Old Harrad.

"Albert Falkenheimer!"

I leaned forward in my desk and tried to say

"Yessir," but my tongue was frozen with fright and all I could muster was a meaningless mumble. Harrad was glaring at me from behind the projector. Its eerie light shone up under his chin, twisting the shadows of his features into something unreal, unnatural, like the face of a villain in a Grade B horror movie. He thrust his head out over the projector towards me, the light catching and reflecting off his glasses so I couldn't see his eyes. I stared at this grotesque face in near-panic.

"Falkenheimer, I don't believe you've heard one word I've said. Please focus your attention on this sentence and tell us"—a wave of his arm included the rest of the class in academic kinship—"which word is the verb?"

My mind was a blank. I heard Henry Schlieff snigger behind my back and felt an impulse to look over at Cathy. But I couldn't. My head refused to move.

Finally I turned my eyes away from Harrad's (grinning?) mask and fixed them on the illuminated screen. Harrad had written *To err is human* in his neat script. If only I could write a fraction as well as that! *Be* was his favourite verb. He could catch most of us with it, and that gave him yet another excuse to lay on with his English accent and conjugate the miserable verb as though he'd invented it himself.

"Come along, Falkenheimer, the verb!" His finger tapped the projector glass impatiently. On the screen a giant black worm raised and lowered its head with each tap. In the near-darkness the monotonous rhythm of the worm's dance punctuated the silence like the regular beat of a metronome.

I managed to free my frozen tongue from the roof of my mouth. "*Is* and *err*," I mumbled.

"Speak up, boy. What are you saying?"

"The verb *to be*," I mumbled a little louder, but Harrad didn't hear me. He gave up with a look of pain on his horror mask and started to peer around for someone who could provide the answer. That was his style. When you couldn't answer a question he'd rub it in by immediately finding someone who could do it without any trouble.

"Sir!" It was Cathy. Now that Harrad's attention was off me I could move my head—released from the sorcerer's spell! Cathy was waving her hand in the air.

"Sir, Falko has it right, I think. He said *is* and *err*. Two verbs, not one." She looked over at me with a smile that I barely caught because my head was caught in the sorcerer's spell again as Harrad turned to me, peering through the half-light.

"That right, Falkenheimer?"

I managed a jerky nod.

"Then speak up, boy!" he barked, his glasses flashing at me.

Now that the pressure was off I could relax. I slumped in my desk and hunched my shoulders against a new blast of icy air from the front of

4

the room while old Harrad started to explain his favourite verb. I sent a grateful grin over to Cathy.

Headline: *Stupid Student Saved Once Again by Lovely Classmate.*

Cathy *is* lovely—at least *I* think she is. We've been going together since grade eight and she's always stuck up for me no matter what, especially whenever I've done something stupid, or frozen, as I did with Harrad.

It was no accident that Cathy was in my English class. Although she didn't like Harrad, she'd bravely dropped Home Ec so her timetable would allow her to take English with me. Somehow she's always managed to be with me in one or two of the academic subjects. This year we were together in English and Science. Since we were partners in Science class she always wrote up the lab reports, so Mr. Parker, the Science teacher, didn't even know I couldn't write properly.

But I couldn't get away with it so easily with old Harrad. My writing filled him with disgust.

"This essay appears to have been written by a chimpanzee, Falkenheimer," he said when I was new in his class. That was the first time I noticed the cold air coming from his desk.

"It's my hand, sir," I mumbled, holding up a thickly bandaged index finger, the sweat starting on my upper lip in spite of the cold.

"Your hand, Albert?"

"Well, my finger, sir." My tongue felt like flannel.

5

"And what is wrong with your finger?"

"Got a bandage on it, sir."

"I can see that for myself, Falkenheimer! *Why* have you a bandage on your finger?"

"I cut it with a bread knife, sir."

As Harrad moved away he muttered something that sounded like "Incompetent fool."

A few sniggers ran around the room. I heard Henry Schlieff behind me echo a whispered "Incompetent fool" and I shivered with the cold.

After that, of course, Harrad inspected my writing often—without the benefit of a phony bandage—and was unimpressed, to put it mildly. He asked me if I was getting help from the Learning Assistance Centre and I told him I was. Schlieff whispered "Retard!" behind my back because the Learning Assistance Centre is for slow kids who have trouble with reading and writing. I don't have as much trouble reading as I used to have, but my writing still needs all the help it can get. So I was spending one period a day at the Centre doing a lot of dumb spelling exercises that don't seem to have done me any good.

In case you haven't already guessed, I've got serious problems when it comes to reading and writing. Shrinks call it dyslexia; people like Schlieff call it stupidity. What it means is that I get letters mixed up. My brain reverses signs and symbols so I end up writing *hlep* instead of *help* and stuff like that.

I've had dyslexia all my life but nobody figured it out until I was in grade six. In the meantime my teachers thought I was just lazy when it came to spelling, and the other kids called me names like "Retard." Naturally I fought back, so my teachers labelled me a troublemaker. The kids just thought I was weird.

Finally I got fed up and one day I wrote a bunch of four-letter words all over the classroom. After that I got sent to a Research Clinic at the University, where a bunch of shrinks tested me and talked to me, tested me again and finally told me I was dyslexic. They also told me that there was no cure for my problem but that I was *obviously* bright enough to overcome it—with a lot of hard work. Imagine! For the first time in my life somebody was telling me that I had a good head on my shoulders. After that my teachers were a bit nicer to me.

My classmates were another story. Now they *knew* I was a retard—certified. And the more special attention I got from my teachers the more I got called names outside class. I began to feel like I had leprosy or something, and I became the class reject. You know, the kid who sits at the back of every classroom, the one you wouldn't be caught dead with in the halls or walking home.

So when Schlieff whispered "Retard!" in Harrad's class a really familiar scene flashed into my mind and began rolling past my eyes like a movie. I can never stop it once it starts. I'm about ten years old. The other kids are yelling and jeering at me in the schoolyard. "Retard!" they're shouting. "Stupid old retard!" The ten-year-old boy

7

lashes out with his fists. There are tears in his eyes. "Retard, retard, retard!" It becomes a chant. The movie hops about madly as if a crowd is jostling the camera. "Retard, retard, retard!" I'm sorry to get melodramatic about this, but even thinking about Schlieff makes me see red.

Anyway, Cathy always stuck up for me, and since Henry was working with her in the Annual Club, he usually went no farther than his whispered insults.

Cathy always helped me out in English, as she did in Science, so my work was a little easier to read. And whenever we got the opportunity she helped me rewrite stuff after school—particularly homework—so I could hand it in the next day. The only other academic subject that gave me any trouble was Social Studies—History, Geography and Current Events—and I had my friend Trivia to help me in that class. Math wasn't too much of a problem. I could write numbers so they were more or less recognizable, and even though Mrs. Cost always complained about the illegible quality of my figures, my untidiness and the way I got addition and multiplication signs mixed up, she didn't treat me too badly.

Cathy was a lifesaver, but I hadn't seen very much of her during school hours so far this year. During the lunch hour she usually went down to Mrs. Cost's room with her friends, snipping pictures for the school Annual, or sometimes she'd go to a Grad Committee meeting in the Art room.

We still saw just as much of each other outside

of school though. Mostly Cathy would come over to my place and we'd sit around talking or watching TV. Sometimes she brought her guitar, my friend Trivia and his sister Doris came over, and we all sang off-key at the top of our lungs.

Mrs. Robinson, Cathy's mother, didn't approve of me until recently. Cathy once told me that she never called me by name—just "that boy with the wild curly hair." Whenever I showed up at their house she had a way of pursing her lips and being very polite that let me know I wasn't at the top of her guest list.

We didn't have this problem at my place. Mom and Dad and Gran always liked having Cathy around, and they seldom asked questions about her. After supper they usually watched TV while Cathy and I sat around listening to records or telling each other bad jokes.

Cathy is pretty: small, with a good figure and long, straight, dark-brown hair, a cute nose and large, truthful brown eyes.

I told her about Old Harrad's refrigeration machine soon after we started our grade ten year, just before she transferred into Harrad's class. It made her laugh.

"Falko, that imagination of yours! Crazy! You make up the wildest things."

"Maybe I do make it all up," I said, a little hurt that she hadn't understood, "but it's real just the same."

"What do you mean? How can it be real?"

"I'm not sure. I just know how I feel. Some-

9

times it's as if I'm an animal in a great big cage. Other times, especially in Harrad's class, I go numb all over and I start to shiver and it seems like there really *is* a machine pumping cold air at me."

Cathy received this in silence, her forehead creased in a tiny frown. Then she reached over and took my hand. "Falko, I wish you wouldn't talk like that. There's no reason for you to feel bad with Harrad or anyone else. Sure you have some problems with reading and writing, but you're smarter than most of the kids in the class. You *must* know that!"

That was Cathy. Always trying to make me feel good, not liking to see me hurt. Even though she could pick her friends from the most popular kids at Carleton High, she spent time with me, making sure I felt okay about myself. Sometimes I wonder what she saw in me! Besides, if I was so smart, why would they be sending me to the Learning Assistance Centre?

Harrad's droning voice broke in on my reverie. "To be. 'To be or not to be: that is the question.' To be. To exist; to live."

Outside in the warm spring sunshine a hand-mower set up a lazy clatter that helped drown out Harrad's voice. I caught a scent of the freshly cut grass as its green spring smell filtered in through the windows and the chinks in the blinds to warm our winter landscape.

* * *

Most days, my favourite activity at school was walking home with Cathy. That day she told me about the Annual she was working on with the other kids, and how they had to keep the costs down by limiting the number of pages.

"It would sure be nice to have those extra blank pages for autographs and year-end comments. But our hands are tied," she explained. "What am I saying? This must all be boring you to death. What about you?"

"Oh, I've been reading more about Houdini—the famous 'Metamorphosis' escape trick. Let me tell you about it—"

"Do I have a choice?"

"No! It went like this. Hands bound together at the wrists, Houdini was put inside a big bag which was tied securely at the top. Then into a trunk which was padlocked and fastened with ropes. In three seconds—just three seconds, think of it!—he escaped. When the trunk was opened and the bag untied, who do you think they found?"

"Fidel Castro?"

"Houdini's wife, Beth, with her hands tied at the wrists. Isn't that something? Cathy, imagine!"

"The mind boggles." Cathy smiled.

"Anyway, this brings me to the good news."

"Good news?"

"I've got an idea for a really modern metamorphosis. With hands and feet tied, in a bag and a locked and tied trunk, I, the Great Falconi, will be placed in a rocket. Three seconds after lift-off I will escape and appear on national television on the Tonight Show. One week later the space capsule, orbiting around the moon, will be opened up. Inside will be found the locked trunk containing—ta-da!—Cathy Robinson, Queen of the Galaxy, conversing with tiny alien life forms, asking them complicated questions about their tiny metabolisms." (Cathy made no secret of her ambitions. She wanted to be a famous biologist, so famous that she'd be invited to accompany space expeditions to the outer reaches of the solar system.)

"Tiny metabolisms, eh? Hey, Falko, speaking of tiny, look at that bikini!" She pointed to a window in Eaton's as we passed through Cedarwood Mall. I looked and saw two skimpy pieces of red silk on a skinny window dummy. "How do you think I'd look in that?" She sucked in her cheeks and struck a bathing-beauty pose.

A picture of Cathy in the red bikini suddenly popped into my mind and I felt my face getting hot.

"Falko, you're blushing!"

"No, I'm not," I lied. "I just got scared for a second. When you stood up straight like that with your hands on your hips you reminded me of the thing from the Barrier Reef in last Friday night's horror movie."

Cathy put her head on my shoulder. "You were blushing. It's no use denying it, Falko, you were *blushing*. Now, I want a straight answer to a question. No fooling around."

She turned and faced me so that I could see her eyes, dark and deep and still.

"Do you like me?" she asked after a pause.

"Like you? Of course I like you. What a question!"

"I mean, do you *really* like me?"

"Yes, I *really* like you."

"How much do you really like me?"

"Aw, Cathy, what kind of a—"

"Do you like me enough that maybe some day we could get married and have kids and go to church and have—"

"Aw, Cathy, have a—"

"Well, *do* you?"

"Okay, okay, I do! Someday we're gonna get—do all the stuff you said. But what's all this got to do with a red bikini?"

Cathy took my hand and pulled me into the store. "Come on, I've got to try it on."

"Try it—"

She came to a halt at the hat department, let go of my hand and slapped on a large, floppy Greta Garbo hat. "Not the bikini, silly, a hat. I love hats. This is how I'll look when we're married and have eight children." She sucked in her cheeks again and rolled her eyes up towards the brim of the hat so that she looked like a *Vogue* cover girl suffering from malnutrition. Then she tried on a couple more hats and dragged me around the store while she modelled a few wigs and umpteen pairs of sunglasses until eventually she'd had enough and was ready to go home.

"Hold it right there, Robinson," I said, trapping her between my outstretched arms. "Now we go try on that red bikini."

"Oh, no!" gasped Cathy. She ducked under my arms and ran for the exit, swerving to avoid the startled shoppers.

Finally I caught up with her outside and we held hands the rest of the way home.

2.

Sometimes I used to get so frustrated that I'd go on what Cathy calls my rampages. Nothing serious—just crazy things like the time I wrote four-letter words all over the classroom. Or my favourite: on the last day of school in grade six I decided that everybody should have a holiday, so I let all the school animals out of their cages. Fourteen mice, five guinea pigs, two rabbits and an iguana, to be precise.

The trouble with these practical jokes was that I usually got caught. I'd forget how recognizable my terrible spelling was and leave what I thought were cryptic messages.

Lately though, when I've been really mad at my teachers or at other kids, I've usually talked it out with Cathy. She understands my feelings better than anybody else and she gives solid advice, even when I don't want to hear it.

But every now and then I get so mad that I *have* to do something about it. I can't explain the anger I feel, but when I get this way Cathy throws up her arms and calls me "Mr. Negative." She figures that nothing she says will stop me—and she's right.

The day after Cathy and I went to Eaton's I arrived at school feeling great. The weather was perfect, it was Friday and I was looking forward to going out with Cathy that night.

But just as I got to my locker I saw something that made my blood boil. Down the hall Manfred McGee, a kid in my homeroom class, was trying to open his combination lock. Manfred wore big, thick glasses and literally worked with his nose in his books. He was so blind that he had to stick his face right against the lock, and even then he took a long time to get it open. That morning he was having a really tough time, mainly because three guys were standing around laughing at him. One of them was Henry Schlieff.

"Hey, Mr. Magoo, what's taking you so long?"

"Dig those crazy shades!"

"You should use your nose to pick the lock. It'd be faster."

Without thinking I walked towards the group.

"Hey, you guys, cut it out!"

"Oh-oh," said Schlieff. "Here comes Retard to save the day. Let's get out of here!"

He and his two friends laughed, but they beat a hasty retreat into homeroom. I'm skinny but tall, and I learned to use my fists a long time ago.

"You okay, Manny?" I asked.

16

"Yeah. I'm used to it." He smiled and shrugged. It was over as far as he was concerned.

As far as *I* was concerned it had just begun. People like Schlieff shouldn't be allowed to get away with terrorizing little guys like Manny.

I sat on my temper all day, but by the time I saw Cathy that night I was ready to kill.

"But Falko, beating up bullies isn't going to do any good. The best thing you can do for Manny is just be his friend. Especially when other people are teasing him."

This *really* made me mad, mainly because it let Henry Schlieff off the hook. So I gave Cathy a long speech about how people should be punished for cruelty. Finally she threw up her hands, called me "Mr. Negative" and said she was leaving. It takes a lot to get Cathy mad, but she sure looked angry when she went out the door.

So much for my Friday night! After Cathy had gone I sat in front of the TV thinking about Manny. He was probably at home studying. He was a good kid who always worked hard and even went out of his way to help other people. Cathy might be mad, but I was madder. I guess I'm a sucker for underdogs. Anyway, I decided to take justice into my own hands.

By Saturday afternoon I'd devised a plan worthy of Houdini: the Locker Caper. And meek, mild-mannered Albert Falkenheimer was about to become "the Falcon."

When it got dark I let myself into the school

17

through the cafeteria window. The lock had been broken for weeks and nobody had bothered to tell the janitor.

I was wearing rubber-soled shoes and thin cotton gloves, and I had a pencil-thin flashlight in my hip pocket. As I walked through the darkened halls I imagined a scene at police headquarters...

The Falcon was the scourge of police all over the world. Scotland Yard, the Sûreté, the FBI and Interpol all had thick dossiers attesting to his coolness and daring. If a valuable diamond necklace was stolen from a rich widow's wall safe on the French Riviera, it was sure to be the Falcon. If valuable negotiable bonds went missing from a safety deposit vault in a Buenos Aires bank, it was undoubtedly the Falcon. If a million dollars worth of securities disappeared from a New York financier's repository, the police knew the Falcon had struck again. He always left his calling card at the scene of the crime. He was hated and feared, envied and respected, internationally.

"Well, Chief Inspector, it looks as though the Falcon has struck again. This time in Vancouver."

"What was stolen, Superintendent?"

"Well, that's the funny part of it—nothing, as far as we can see." The Superintendent sat drumming his fingers on the edge of the desk, his expression a combination of baffled amazement, hopeless despair and fatigue.

In the school office I found the locker cards for Division 26—where my homeroom class's lockers were—without too much trouble and took them up to the second floor. Don't ask me how I got into the office. Let's just say I've spent a lot of time studying Houdini's tricks.

Reading the combinations off the cards, I removed all the locks from the locker doors—my own and Manfred's included, for obvious reasons. Then I mixed them up and snapped them back on different doors. I left one locker door open—the one directly opposite the door to Division 26 homeroom.

Then I went into Mrs. Cost's room next door and got the key for the equipment room from her desk drawer. I took a cassette recorder from the shelf in the equipment room, locked the door again and returned the key to Mrs. Cost's drawer.

Taking a cassette from my jacket pocket, I slipped it into the recorder, which I then put in the open locker outside our homeroom. I attached a simple time switch to the recorder and set it to start playing the tape at nine o'clock Monday morning. Then I closed the locker, securing it with a lock taken from one of the other lockers.

Back at the office I returned the locker cards to the file and took the combination index and hid it under the cushion of the vice-principal's chair. I let myself out of the school the same way I had got in. I hadn't seen a soul. Everything had gone according to plan.

The time switch was first-rate. I'd made it myself and Mr. Jackson, who teaches Electricity, thinks I'm really good at electronics. He gave me an A, the only one I've ever had in my life. I like Mr. Jackson.

On Monday morning we all stood outside waiting for the 8:45 bell. When it went, six hundred kids surged into the hallways to begin another week of mind-boggling boredom.

Upstairs on the second floor my homeroom "pals" struggled to open unresponsive combination locks.

"What's the matter with this lock? It won't open."

"Yeah, mine too. That's funny!"

"Stop crowdin' me!"

"Who d'you think you're shovin'?"

Curses and angry shouts, pushing and fighting —pandemonium in the hallway as the twenty-five students of Division 26 yelled and jostled and fought, pulling at locks and locker doors that refused to obey the usual combinations. Other kids from up and down the hall began to come over to see what all the excitement was about, adding to the noise and confusion. Finally Mr. Bird, the vice-principal, came up to investigate.

"What's going on here?"

Henry Schlieff appointed himself spokesman. "Dunno, sir. We can't get our locks open."

"This your locker, Schlieff?" asked Mr. Bird.

"Yessir."

"What's your combination?"

"38-23-59."

Big Bird tried the numbers. The lock refused to open. He started to get mad. "Get into your homeroom at once. This will be investigated."

By this time Mr. Factori, our homeroom teacher, had arrived and he began to bellow and wave his arms around "Everybody into class!"

The kids moved into homeroom slowly, reluctantly, pointing back at their lockers. "But we haven't got no books or nuthin'. We can't go to class without no books!" Kids always use atrocious grammar in front of teachers, just to get them mad.

"Inside," yelled Big Bird, his normally dough-coloured face now the colour of wild blueberries.

The bell signalling the end of homeroom and the beginning of the first class of the day rang a minute after we all got inside, so everyone jumped up again and took off, giving old Factori no time to take attendance.

I quickly made my way down to the end of the corridor to Room 24, Mr. Platt's Socials class. It was precisely 8:59. Everybody was waiting for Platypus to begin the boredom.

One minute later the quiet of the upper floor was shattered by a loud *Da-da-da-da*. The tape I'd slipped into the recorder had begun to play the opening bars of *Beethoven's Fifth Symphony*. It boomed out loud and strong from the locker opposite Factori's open door.

Platt went to his door to see what the disturbance was all about. Big Bird had been writing down the serial numbers of the locks on the sabotaged lockers, to check their combinations in the index, but now he moved to the Beethoven locker so he could open it quickly and turn off the Berlin Philharmonic Orchestra. Factori was there too, waving his arms at Big Bird and bellowing in a deep baritone that Beethoven would have appreciated.

By now a lot of kids had followed their teachers out into the hall, and once more bedlam ensued as the Berlin Philharmonic competed with the shouts and laughter of two hundred overjoyed students.

At 9:30 the Beethoven tape ran out and order was more or less restored.

I passed the offending locker as I changed classes for period two. The door was open and there was no sign of the tape recorder. Big Bird must have found the combination list under his cushion or had the janitor cut the lock off the door. Who cared? My plan had succeeded brilliantly.

The Chief Inspector leaned forward in his swivel chair and fixed the Superintendent with an incredulous stare. "Did you say that nothing was taken, sir?"

"Yes, that's the part we don't understand. Why would the infamous Falcon break into a high school just to change twenty-five combination locks around? Why would he play a tape of the first movement of a Beethoven symphony? Why was nothing taken? Why? Why?" The Superin-

tendent threw his hands into the air in baffled rage.

"Hmmm," mused the Chief Inspector. "Which symphony was it?"

"The Fifth."

"The Fifth? Hmmmm. Must be something to it."

"Chief, bring me a list of the serial numbers of those locks. I want the numbers and combinations. Then contact Schmidt in Berlin and have him go over that tape with a fine-toothed comb. Tell him top priority. There's something very fishy about this whole thing. I have a feeling that unless we break it—and break it quick—we're going to be in real trouble."

"Yes, sir," gasped the Chief Inspector as he scrambled to his feet.

"And Chief!"

"Sir?"

"Not a word of this to the Press. I want Security A Plus on this one! The Falcon may be able to make fools of everyone else, but the Vancouver Police Department is a cat of a different colour!"

"Horse, sir!"

"Get on it, Chief."

"Yes, sir."

That afternoon just before dismissal bell at 3:30 Mr. Frost, the principal, came on the PA and sounded off about the whole thing. He demanded that the person or persons responsible for "the

23

immature practical joke" give themselves up. He wanted to make himself perfectly clear about this (Frost always sounded like Richard Nixon on the PA). Any students having any information as to the identity of the culprit or culprits must come forward immediately. The whole joke was in the worst possible taste and made a mockery of the best traditions of Carleton High . . .

I was above suspicion. Hadn't my lock been changed too? And anyway, everyone knew that a Retard couldn't pull off a caper like that! I hoped Manfred was enjoying it all.

I felt a warm glow of pleasure as I sat listening to Mr. Frost and waiting, like Ferlinghetti, for the new birth of freedom in British Columbia.

3.

"Falkenheimer!"

For a second I didn't know where I was or who the voice belonged to. I'd seen a movie the night before, a collection of film clips from the twenties with great comedians like Chaplin, Keaton and Lloyd. They were all throwing pies at each other and I was thinking about the people I'd like to see with custard all over their faces. Harrad, for starters. Or Mrs. Cost and her lunch-hour Annual browners.

"Falkenheimer! Are you sleeping again?"

Room 402 suddenly came into focus and I realized the voice was Harrad's. He was walking down the aisle towards me tossing a piece of chalk in his hand. This time he'd really caught me off guard and the expression on his face was triumphant. A cold blast began to pump out from the refrigeration machine and I shivered. Harrad held the chalk out in front of him.

"To the board, Falkenheimer. We'll see how you do at dictation. Quickly!"

I took the chalk and stood up in a daze, glancing at Cathy for reassurance. The other kids had all wakened and looked interested in the possible diversion. As I made my way to the board I heard Henry Schlieff whisper something. I couldn't hear it but I knew what it was, and I clenched the chalk in a tight fist.

Harrad dictated a short, simple sentence and I started to write, accidentally squeaking the chalk and, as usual, getting the spelling all wrong. Then the chalk fell from my frozen fingers.

Harrad exploded. "Enough, enough, Falkenheimer! Sit down, boy. Janice, finish it off!" Cathy touched my hand as I stumbled back to my desk.

I spent the rest of the class twisting and turning in my seat. If I sat up straight my knees jammed under the desktop. If I slid down so I was sitting on my spine, my legs shot forward under Louise Potter's desk and got caught in the wire bookrack under her chair. Louise thought I was deliberately knocking her desk to get her attention and she giggled so loud it made Harrad stare at me.

"Falkenheimer, since you insist on bothering other people in class I suppose you're bored with your work. See me at the end of class and I'll assign you a few more challenging exercises."

I opened my mouth to explain but Harrad turned his back before anything came out. By now I was thinking of throwing more than pie in his face . . .

* * *

My next class was Music with Mrs. Powell, who was getting hysterical about our big class project. This year it was the closest thing we'd ever done to a rock musical—based loosely on *The Rose,* the musical about Janis Joplin.

We were just a few weeks away from dress rehearsal and Mrs. Powell was beginning to realize that we would never sound like professional musicians. The fact that our audience would consist only of parents and friends didn't seem to calm her down.

Usually I got along okay with Mrs. Powell, but that morning I was pretty upset already and I went too far. My mistake was making jokes during the class. I didn't notice just how edgy Mrs. Powell was. I was standing in the chorus whispering to Trivia when the axe fell.

"Albert Falkenheimer, I've asked you to be quiet four times today and I'm not going to ask you again. Since you don't want to work in this production you can consider yourself out of it. And you can explain why to Mr. Bird this afternoon."

Her voice was shaking. It was definitely too late to say I was sorry and I broke out in a cold sweat at the prospect of trying to explain to Big Bird. Maybe I was still upset about Harrad, I don't know. But as I passed Mrs. Powell I muttered something I shouldn't have.

She turned a deep red. "You can also explain *that* to Mr. Bird!"

* * *

27

After a morning like that I had to talk to Cathy. But when I got to the cafeteria at lunch time she was surrounded by her Annual cronies and Mrs. Cost was busy giving them instructions.

I sat in a corner watching them until they finally broke apart. Cathy came right over to me, took me by the arm and led me out into the schoolyard. The frown on her face meant I was going to get a lecture. "Falko," she began when we'd found a shady spot under a tree, "don't let Harrad get to you like that. His bark's worse than his bite—"

"I know, I *know!* But I can't help it." I punched at the tree and winced as a sharp pain ran through my hand. "I keep thinking he's going to say something like—well, like I'm stupid. In front of the whole class."

Cathy had taken my hand. The skin was broken in a couple of places and she began to dab them with a handkerchief.

"You've got to control your temper. And whatever Harrad does to you, you shouldn't take it out on Mrs. Powell. Everybody knows she's as nervous as anything."

"Aw, come on, Cathy. I didn't mean to bug her. I was just—"

"Letting off steam, I know. But you can't keep on doing it whenever you feel frustrated."

"Listen, that's easy for you to say. You don't have to deal with—"

"Well, well, if it isn't Harrad's favourite English student." Henry Schlieff had come up behind me. He looked at my bleeding hand and then at Cathy.

"You ready, Cath?" he asked.

"Yeah, you go ahead. I'll catch up with you." Cathy watched him walk away and then looked me straight in the eye. "Falko, I can't talk now. Mrs. Cost has given us a new deadline for the Annual and we've really got to rush. Henry's going to show us the club pictures he's taken so we can do the write-ups for them."

"Can I see you after school?"

"Sorry, but we're going to be working late today. I'll call you. Take care."

Then she was gone, running across the school yard after Schlieff. It was the last straw. Next to Harrad, Henry was the biggest threat to mankind. I wondered what kind of pie I'd use on him.

* * *

Big Bird deliberately kept people waiting outside his office. It heightened the fear and suspense. Even though I knew this, I still felt nervous. The vice-principal's job was to keep discipline among the students, and his specialty was dealing with the problem kids like me.

There was one other kid sitting on the bench outside the office. His name was Kirby Something-or-other, from grade eight. He looked like he had the makings of a real hood: thin, pale face; fat, protruding lower lip; greasy hair that fell into his eyes and that he didn't bother to push back; jean jacket and pants. His T-shirt had a marijuana motif.

He turned to me sullenly, eyes staring through a curtain of hair. "What they got you on?"

I shrugged. I couldn't let a grade eight kid see that I was worried. "Mouthing off to a teacher, I guess." After a short silence in which Kirby digested this information, I asked politely, "What about you?"

His eyes lit up behind their curtain. "The works! Six class lates, smoking in the can, opening my locker between periods—and I think they got me on a skipping-out rap." He flashed me a superior grin. I wondered where he'd picked up the jailhouse talk. Probably from watching old Cagney movies on TV. His grin faded. "You know, this place is like a prison. Rules for everything. Everywhere you go out of class you have to have an administration slip. 'Get out of your locker, boy!' 'What are you doing in the hall, boy?' I'm sick of it. Up to here! You'd think we was in the big house or something."

Big Bird's door opened and a sullen grade nine girl walked by without a glance at us. Big Bird scowled at Kirby. "You're next, Taylor. In you go."

Kirby slouched into the office followed by Big Bird, who turned to scowl at me too before closing the door.

I tried to relax. In the outer office the two secretaries went on with their work as if I didn't exist. Maybe I didn't. I closed my eyes, trying to imagine non-existence, but all I could see were gargoyle faces hissing "Retard!" at me.

The brittle buzz of two voices raised in argument suddenly came from the office next to Big Bird's—the principal's office. Mr. Frost sounded—not mad exactly, but a little angry or hurt. It was the tone of voice my mother uses sometimes when she feels she's been treated badly by my father. I strained to hear what Frost was saying.

"But Mrs. Powell, it's not only doubtful *legally,* it's unsound *ethically.*"

"You okayed the outline over a month ago. You made no objections about the suitability of the music then."

"Mrs. Powell, I assumed you would procure the necessary performance rights. I *assumed* it. There *is* such a thing as copyright, you know!"

"For a high school production? The costs would be more than the production could afford."

"Nonetheless I assumed it, Mrs. Powell. I know it's too late at this stage to make changes. I only hope there are no repercussions."

"What could happen? Do you think a big New York publishing company like Farr and Krauss would stoop to suing a small Canadian high school? I really think you're being a bit too cautious. High schools mount musicals and dramas all the time. Think of the costs if every song or piece of music had to be paid for! Besides, it's not as if we're making a profit."

"I question only the ethics of such a point of view, Mrs. Powell."

The voices went on. Fancy that! The school musical! I didn't know what the rights and wrongs of copyright were, but it'd sure be funny if Mrs. Powell got sued. It would serve her right for telling me off in front of all those kids. I could just see a letter arriving from the big important publisher or a New York law firm.

Dear Mrs. Powell,
It has come to our attention that on such-and-such a date you infringed copyright numbers so-and-so, such copyrights being the sole property of Messrs. So-and-so of Such-a-place, New York.

The name of the publisher would be on the scores in the music room. Farr and Something. Inspiration had struck! I could invent a name, get a lettering set—the kind you rub over with your pencil—from the drafting room and easily forge a letterhead. Trivia could help me with the spelling and type the letter. The problem would be mailing it. It would need a U.S. stamp to look authentic.

Then I remembered my cousin Wendy in Buffalo. That was in New York State—close enough, even though it wasn't New York City. Who would notice? The postmark would say New York and the stamps would be American! That would be good enough.

Big Bird's door opened and Kirby lurched out

with a grin on his face. Bird beckoned to me, his Pillsbury Doughboy face creased in a frown of disapproval. What about pumpkin pie right in the middle of that miserable face? It would match his complexion. Inside, I sat tensely while he bawled me out and gave me three after-school detentions for impertinence to a teacher.

That night Trivia helped me put the letter and the letterhead together and we celebrated by going to McDonald's. On the way I mailed it off to Wendy.

4.

You can always tell when it's a weekend—it always seems to rain. That Saturday morning was soaking wet, so I did what I always do on rainy weekends. I went over to Trivia's.

Trivia's real name is Tracy Spencer Johnson. He has two older, out-of-school twin brothers named Bogart and Cagney, and one sister, Doris Day Johnson. In case you didn't guess, Trivia's parents are film freaks. So is Trivia. But more than that, he's a walking encyclopedia. Not just movies, but historical and scientific stuff—any kind of trivia.

I guess I've known him as long as I've known anybody. We started school together. The only difference was that I stayed at the same elementary school for seven years while Trivia must have been in a dozen during the same time. His family was always moving. How we remained friends is hard to understand except that he seemed to reappear every year or so. Apart from spending eight months in my grade-one class, he was in my grade-six class for five months and my grade-seven class for a few weeks. In between he seemed to have attended all the nearby schools as well as having been enrolled in about five different ones when his family lived in Saskatchewan for a year.

He moved twice after starting at Carleton High but decided to keep coming to Carleton even though he lived outside the school's boundaries. He liked being in the Projectionist Club, where he could indulge his love of film. That, in fact, was all he did in school. His marks were usually almost as lousy as mine, but he always put in a little effort near the end of the year and scraped through.

Trivia had one distinct advantage over me: he wrote beautifully. And he could read. Not only that, he *liked* to read. He wore huge sunglasses and was generally looked on as a genius who could get high marks if he felt like it. The chances of Trivia being placed in the Learning Centre for remedial exercises were about the same as the Rolling Stones playing at the next Carleton sock hop.

His school attendance this year was much better than it used to be. Although he still liked to skip out every so often to see a movie, he was much more selective than before. I went with him whenever there was something on that interested me. A nice break from Harrad and company.

Doris, Trivia's sister, is a year younger than us,

but she's been in the same grade as us for years because she skipped grade five. This happened when her wandering family stayed for a few months in one of the more remote communities of the province. It had a one-room school and not enough grade-five materials, so Doris just shared Trivia's grade-six books and ended up passing grade six.

This doesn't mean that Doris is really smarter than Trivia. It means that she's more organized. She's also, despite being a bit overweight and affecting a hard-rock manner (*Repulsive Pictures proudly presents Doris "Hard Rock" Johnson in* I Was a Teenage Gun Moll), quite athletic. Doris often used to skip out with us.

Whenever we skipped out to go to the movies we'd get some mince pies and sausage rolls to eat in the theatre. Reid's was a butcher shop the three of us sort of stumbled into one day. Maybe it was its Scottish motto taken from one of Robert Burns' poems—"We hae meat that ye can eat"—that made us check it out. As soon as those elaborately scrolled words had imprinted their message on Trivia's computer brain, he'd adopted an accent as thick and plaintive as a set of bagpipes winding down slowly in a vat of porridge. Before you could say "haggis," he'd linked arms with Doris, who's about as Scottish-looking as Liza Minnelli, and was doing a little jig as he propelled her through the revolving doors. I followed in their wake with the confidence of an ant at an aardvark convention. Even the usually unflappable Doris looked a little embarrassed when Trivia ordered some "bonnie wee pies fur ma bonnie wee sisterrr." We decided that Reid's pies were the greatest, much better than soggy popcorn, fossilized chocolate bars or shoe-leather burgers. And the place looked like a shop out of time with its sawdust-strewn floor, huge smelly cheeses and hickory-cured hams. Perfect if we were on our way to a horror movie.

Armed with our goodies, we always headed for a tacky, second-rate cinema called the Empire. The Empire, which had been declining and falling since the twenties, was run by a nattily dressed little man whose black, slicked-back hair had more oil potential than the Athabasca Tar Sands. He always wore a tuxedo with a big red carnation in the lapel and patrolled the lobby proudly, as if it was Radio City Music Hall.

Unfortunately, this impressive façade couldn't cover up his complete ignorance of movies. He gave some real turkeys top billing and downgraded great classics. He once teamed the Academy Award-winning *Space Odyssey* with a cheap sci-fi flick, *The Earth Died Screaming* (a fate that should have been shared by the producers), and made the latter the main attraction. But nobody cared because the Empire always showed double bills at cheap prices. It also offered a lot of revivals of old comedies—Laurel and Hardy, Abbott and Costello, the Marx Brothers and even silents like Chaplin and Keaton.

Going to the Empire with Trivia and Doris was

like a renewal—a cleansing. I could escape my meek, mild existence to become Count Falko, the debonair swordsman and man of honour; Buck Falko, fastest gun west of the Pecos; or the mysterious Falko, clouding men's minds and rooting out the weed of crime at every opportunity. Sometimes, though, even when the three of us were laughing, cracking jokes or passing comments, I saw myself as somebody else: Buster Falko, the sad clown—the lonely little guy whose frantic, mechanical motions were as overdone as his hastily applied makeup.

I didn't mean to go into all this. It's just that the Empire brings back some of my richest memories from high school. That rainy Saturday morning when I went over to Trivia's, all I wanted to do was forget. Forget school, forget that I'd had a fight with my parents, forget that Cathy hadn't called me for two whole days.

Trivia's house was a completely disorganized mess. The doors were always open and it always looked like nobody was home. His parents usually weren't. Both of them worked on weekends cleaning office buildings. I saw somebody in the kitchen—Doris. Bogart and Cagney were probably out terrorizing the neighbourhood.

"Where's Trivia?" I asked.

Doris was stirring something that looked like a cross between porridge and soup. "He's downstairs." She squinted in my direction. She's always needed glasses but wouldn't wear them even if she got them. They'd spoil her greaser image. "You want some stew?" The ooze in the pot gurgled menacingly.

"No thanks. I just want to see Trivia."

Trivia's room in the basement is a shrine. You feel you should take your shoes off before entering. As I went down the stairs I could hear the nasal whine of Fred Allen one-upping Jack Benny. Trivia collects old radio tapes.

"Hi, Falko. This is a great one. Have a seat."

Half of his face was hidden behind huge aviator-style lenses. No wonder Doris was paranoid about wearing glasses.

He put his earphones back on and listened. I sat down and waited. There was no use trying to interrupt him while he was listening to *Allen's Alley, Inner Sanctum, Suspense Theatre* or any other golden oldies.

When the tape eventually ran out, Trivia sat back, whisked off his headphones and turned off the machine. "That was a great one, Falko. I've been waiting for Cullen to play it again for over six months." Missing Jack Cullen's nostalgic radio show was sacrilege to Trivia.

"So what's buzzin', cousin?" His vocabulary is full of corny expressions he picks up from the old tapes and movies he wallows in.

I shrugged. "What do you say we go downtown to the Community Centre? We could rent skates and try out the rink."

"Good idea!" Trivia jumped to his feet.

"Doris," he yelled up the stairs, "you coming?"

"Coming where?"

"Ice skating."

"Sure, why not? This stew's a dead loss anyway."

The ice rink at the Community Centre is surrounded by a sort of drop-in, sit-down, coffeehouse restaurant. Kids from Carleton and other schools lounge around drinking pop and munching chips. Don Harris, the director, makes sure there's nothing stronger than soft drinks around, and usually there isn't because the kids respect him. Sometimes I wish some of my teachers were like him.

When we got there the rink was almost empty. A crowd was gathering around Don, who was trying to create some interest in a skating contest. "Look, kids, we need some more couples to round out the contest. Anybody can enter. We've got some great prizes: a book of movie passes, some McDonald's certificates and a twenty-dollar Sears coupon."

"Falko, why don't you and Doris enter?" asked Trivia. "You're both good skaters. I'd do it too, but you know I skate like an epileptic emu."

It's true that I'm not a bad skater. One of the gym teachers back in elementary school wanted me to try out for a peewee hockey team. But I didn't bother because I didn't want the coach yelling at me every time I got left and right mixed up, which you do if you're dyslexic, especially when you have to follow directions and

40

make quick decisions. I used to skate about once a week, usually with Trivia or some of the other kids from school. Sometimes when I felt depressed I went by myself. Skating was an escape. The old arena where we used to go was pretty run down but the surface of the ice was so smooth that when you got moving it was as though you were flying. I really like that feeling! Your feet lose touch with the ground and your mind switches onto automatic pilot. I sometimes found it hard to come down from those flights, though one day my landing was quicker than expected.

I was passing a girl who moved with the jerky self-consciousness of a novice skater. She must have bumped me as I was passing because suddenly my skates seemed to go off in opposite directions and I hit the ice.

"Hey, are you okay?" She reached down cautiously to make sure I was still alive. "I'm just learning. Sorry I tripped you up like that."

That was how I met Cathy. We often saw each other at the arena after that although we didn't start going around together until much later.

She eventually became a good skater. She really worked at it as a skill to be mastered and not, like me, as a means of escape. Trivia, on the other hand, never mastered skating because he had a habit of looking down and crashing into the walls. Doris always lacked style but she more than made up for it with stamina. Watching her skate you got the impression that she was trying to break through the ice instead of glide over it.

Before I could answer Trivia and refuse to have anything to do with Don Harris's skating contest, I heard an all-too-familiar voice in the crowd.

"Look, Cathy, it's a cinch. All these yo-yos are losers. They can't skate. We'll skate 'em into the ice!"

I glanced quickly in the direction of the voice. It was Henry Schlieff with Cathy and the Annual crowd. She shook her head and pointed to her ankle, but my blood still boiled at the thought of her skating with Schlieff.

"Okay," I said. "Let's skate. What have we got to lose?"

"That's what I like," answered Doris, pretending to sulk. "An enthusiastic partner!"

We got our skates and went over to the far end of the rink where Don Harris was explaining the rules.

"Okay, everybody, no rough stuff like tripping or shoving. Right, Joey?" A big greaser in a studded leather jacket grinned knowingly. "This is an endurance skateathon." Don loves to tack "athon" on all his activities. He's sponsored danceathons, sleepathons and even eatathons.

"You're gonna skate to music," he continued. "First it'll be a slow and dreamy waltz." Boos. "Then we'll pick up the tempo with some fast rock." Cheers. "You've gotta keep the pace. Those who can't, or those who fall, are out. Remember, this is a team effort and you must hold on to your partner's hand at all times. That shouldn't be too tough, eh, Joey?" Scattered laughter. "Any questions? Good! As soon as you're ready, line up here and we'll start."

There was a flurry of activity from the twenty couples taking part. Spectators began to line the sides of the rink. Schlieff caught sight of us. He'd finally found someone—Madeleine Armstrong, one of the Annual Club girls—to be his partner. He said something to her and they both laughed. I looked for Cathy but couldn't see her anywhere.

Doris skated over to me. "You all set, Falko?"

"Sure."

Trivia was now at rinkside. I took off my jacket and tossed it to him.

Doris reached over to me. "You wanna stick of gum?"

I nodded. Doris should be on the board of the Wrigley Corporation the way she passes out samples. "Can you skate and chew gum at the same time?" I asked her. Just then Schlieff skated over and braked nonchalantly in a small shower of ice.

"You think you stand a chance against me, Philco, when I've got a real skating partner instead of a female Fonz?" He sometimes called me Philco because of my good grades in Electricity.

Doris, busy relacing one of her boots, heard this last crack. "Female Fonz, huh?" She smiled. "How about a date in a dark alley sometime, big boy?"

Henry was so embarrassed she'd heard him that he did something out of character: he blushed. "Aw, forget it, Doris. I was only kidding."

"You've made your point, Schlieff," I snapped. "Now flake off!"

"Okay, Philco. Hope you can skate without an extension cord." With that he slithered back to Madeleine.

Doris had finally got her skates adjusted to her liking. "Don't let Henry get to you, Falko." She smiled as she stood up. "We'll do all right."

Don was becoming impatient. "C'mon, kids, let's line up. We haven't got all day. Spread out. Let's make it a good straight line."

We squeezed in next to a couple with a severe case of terminal acne. I thought *I* was nervous, but those two kids looked as if they were going through the final agonies of fatal stage fright.

"Poor kids," whispered Doris. She offered them some gum and the assurance that everyone in the contest was nervous.

"On your marks, get ready—skate!"

We were off to the strains of something that would have decarbonated Lawrence Welk's bubble machine. We did a few slow circles and glides and I began to relax a little. It wasn't as crowded as I'd thought it would be.

Suddenly the music switched to a faster tempo. "C'mon, kids, pick it up! Faster! Faster!" barked Don.

I tightened my grip on Doris's hand and we started to dodge in and out of the other couples. I could see Schlieff up ahead doing some fancy turns with Madeleine, but some of the other kids were tiring already. Don must have got this skateathon idea from watching *They Shoot Horses, Don't They?*

One couple fell. Another ran into the railing. Then the music slowed down again, but I found it hard to slacken my pace.

"Take it easy, Falko," puffed Doris. "If you keep this up you'll tire yourself out. I've got enough trouble pushing myself around without pulling you."

Trivia gave us a thumbs up salute as we passed him.

Then I caught sight of Cathy. She was watching Schlieff and Madeleine, but when she saw me she waved and yelled something. It was drowned out by the noise of the crowd.

"Hey, what's with you, Falko? First I can't get you to slow down and now you're moving like a sick turtle wearing concrete overshoes."

The music picked up again and more couples were eliminated. My legs were starting to feel rubbery. My hands and Doris's were no longer separate entities. Maybe we'd spend the rest of our lives like this (*Repulsive Pictures proudly presents* The Incredible Two-Headed Arctic Ice Fiend).

The spectators were beginning to blur as we circled the rink once again. When I checked my watch I found we'd been skating for forty-five minutes. I shook my head and realized there were only three couples left: us, Schlieff and Madeleine, and the couple with terminal acne.

I glanced at Doris. In her leather jacket she looked a bit like an overdone baked potato. The acne couple seemed pretty well beat too, though it was hard to know how much their redness of face was due to physical exertion and how much to their natural complexions. Schlieff and Madeleine showed some signs of fatigue like the rest of us, but they were still setting a fast pace. It looked like we were going to be here for some time yet.

Suddenly Schlieff and Madeleine made a quick swerve in front of the acne couple. "Henry's not fighting fair," said Doris in dismay. The acne couple were knocked off balance but managed to recover—barely.

Schlieff and Madeleine circled again. As long as they didn't actually touch the other couple they couldn't be disqualified. "They're going to go after them again," puffed Doris. "Then they'll try the same thing on us if we're still around."

Schlieff started to move up to pass us. Doris squeezed my hand hard (I'd thought it was devoid of feeling) and mumbled something about "jungle time." Just as Schlieff and Madeleine were about to pass, Doris opened her mouth and let out a yell that would have made Tarzan cringe. Having a partner from a family of movie freaks has its advantages.

The ten-point Richter Scale crumbled. The sudden noise had caught the Schlieff duet completely off guard. They swerved, clipped us, tried to regain control, but Schlieff lost his balance. He fell over the rink railing, pulling Madeleine with him.

The distraction of Schlieff's unexpected exit was too much for me. I failed to notice the rapidly approaching railing at the other end of the rink and despite a frantic tug from Doris we sailed over it.

"You okay, Falko?" she moaned.

"I will be when you get off my back and take your skate out of my nose!" I struggled to a sitting position and looked around the rink. "Did the acne couple survive your Schlieff shatterer?"

"You bet!" she laughed. "They won!"

Don hurried over. "You kids all right?"

We nodded.

"I saw what Henry and Madeleine were up to, but they were within the rules. You helped Billy and Jane win and they're really excited! I'm glad. You know, they didn't want to enter the contest because they were afraid they weren't good enough." Don laughed. "I thought Henry and Madeleine had it all sewn up until you gave that yell. Does the city zoo know about you?"

When Don left I turned to Doris. "Okay, Hard Rock! You made up your mind to watch out for the acne twins after you gave 'em some gum at the starting line and saw how nervous they were. You're a phony, Doris! Underneath that leather jacket you're one hundred percent marshmallow!"

A slow blush spread across Doris's cheeks and

she laughed. "Yeah, well right now I'm a melted marshmallow. Let's get these skates off and get out of here before the custodial crew mops me up."

Just then Cathy ran over. "I wondered if you two were all right, but judging from the noise you're making you'll live. Henry and Madeleine aren't too happy, but I'm glad those other kids won. Here." Cathy had my coat. "Trivia gave me this. He's on his way over with some hot chocolate." She helped me on with my coat.

"Howdie, stranger," I said. "Want to walk a hero home?"

Doris discreetly moved away to find Trivia.

"Oh Falko, I'm sorry, but we've got to work on the Annual this afternoon. Mrs. Cost wants all the picture captions by next week."

I looked down at my feet and then back up at Cathy's face. Her work on the Annual was beginning to sound like an excuse for not seeing me, but her eyes were as warm and honest as ever. Besides, this was hardly the place to ask her if she was trying to dump me.

She seemed to sense that I was upset. "Listen, I'll call you tomorrow ... "

"Promise?"

"Promise."

5.

Cathy called me, all right, and I went over to her place on Sunday night. Even though it was pouring rain and the next day was Monday, I whistled and hummed all the way. Cathy had been acting kind of distant lately—maybe because of all my griping and practical joking—but I'd make it up with her somehow, I thought. I always did.

Was I ever in for a surprise. That night I found out we were finished. The end. And the worst part of it was she was dumping me to go out with Henry Schlieff.

This I just couldn't understand. Sure, Henry is probably what any girl would call good-looking, maybe even handsome, but his personality is—to put it as kindly as possible—creepy. How could she be taken in by his syrupy smile? All he ever talked about was himself: his prowess at basketball, his being top of the class in Phys Ed, his school record for the 800 metres and his camera work for the Annual.

If looks and athletic ability were what really counted in life, then Cathy had got herself a genuine bargain. Henry was tall and muscular, with broad shoulders, while I was only tall and skinny. My shoulders looked like matchsticks. Henry had tidy, auburn hair, wavy and thick. My hair was too long—wild and bristly, the colour and texture of straw, and it looked like I'd been watching Frankenstein movies all my life. Henry's teeth were white and even. Mine were indifferently scattered around my mouth with two big gaps so that if I opened my mouth and clenched my teeth you'd still be able to see my uvula waving around at the back of my throat. Henry's eyes were blue; mine were an indeterminate shade of green with a smidgin or two of cholera-yellow mixed in. Henry's nose was straight, mine bent. The truth was, compared to me Henry looked like a Greek god.

And, of course, he was a solid "B" academic student, not a struggling "Pass." Not to mention the fact that, while most of my friends were rejects, Henry hung around with the most popular kids in school.

But I'm getting ahead of myself. That Sunday night I knew something was wrong as soon as Mrs. Robinson answered my knock on the door.

"Well, hello, Albert!" She appeared surprised and flustered, unlike her usual calm, disdainful self. She didn't ask me in, which was also kind of strange. Instead, she turned and called back into the house, "Cathy, it's Albert, dear." Then she faced me again, keeping her hand on the door-knob. "How is your mother?" She flashed her teeth at me.

I mumbled to her. Cathy came to the door and relieved her mother, the gatekeeper.

"Come in, Falko." I followed her along the short hallway and into Mr. Robinson's den where he kept his Book-of-the-Month collection. He must have been collecting them for years because the whole wall, right to the ceiling, was papered with books of the month.

I threw myself into the easy chair next to the book-lined wall. Cathy sat on the ottoman near the chair.

"What's with your mother?" I asked.

"Mom? What do you mean?"

"How come she's being so polite to me? I didn't even know she could smile."

"Oh, stop it." Cathy didn't look as amused as she usually did when I made cracks about her mother. "You always see her bad side."

"Is there another one?" I meant it to be funny, but as soon as I said it I knew it was wrong.

Cathy glared at me. "If that's your idea of a joke, maybe she's right. I mean, you're always putting people down. When they *are* nice to you, why can't you just accept it?"

"Hold it right there. What's this about 'maybe she's right'? Is there something I should know?"

"No. Just—"

"*Just?*"

"Well, you know. What every mother says. 'Do

you really like him?' 'How are his grades?' 'Are you sure you should see so much of him—'"

"So *much* of me! Cathy, I've hardly seen you lately. You're so damn busy with the Annual."

"It happens to be important to me. If you can't understand that, maybe we *should* stop seeing each other—at least the way we have been."

I sat in stunned silence for a minute. Mrs. Robinson had never liked me, but Cathy had always stood up for me. I couldn't figure out why she wasn't doing it now. Then a light went on in my brain.

"Does this have anything to do with Henry Schlieff?" I had to know.

Cathy looked down at the floor. I could tell by her silence that I'd hit a nerve. But before I could say anything her mother came in, as if on cue.

"Would Albert like some lemonade? I just made some fresh." That was a switch. The only things Mrs. Robinson had ever offered me before were cool sarcasm and disapproving glances.

"No thanks, I'm just about to leave," I mumbled. She must have felt the tension in the room because she quickly retreated to the hall.

"Looks like rain," she called as she closed the door.

I turned back to Cathy. "So I was right." I'm sure my face was pale. I felt sick, and Cathy didn't look much better. Her eyes were misty. I hoped she wasn't going to cry. I should have got up right then and left, but there seemed to be a devil inside me goading me on to commit verbal suicide. I heard myself saying, "Why Schlieff? Anybody but him! Why couldn't you pick a human being instead of an idiot like him?"

"Don't say things like that," Cathy responded loyally, her eyes beginning to flash with anger. "Henry may act like a snob, but underneath he's the same as anybody else. I like him.

"Falko, just think for a minute," she added more calmly. "We've been going together for two years now—almost three—and Mom feels it's wrong for me to be seeing so much of you. Maybe she *is* right. Maybe we should cool it for a while whether or not one of us is interested in somebody else. I should meet other boys and you should meet other girls. You get a wider experience of life and people that way. And we can still be friends." She paused for breath.

I should have known Mrs. Robinson would get to her eventually. But I wasn't going to say anything angry. That would be making it too easy for Cathy.

"Anyway, look who's talking about being an idiot," she continued. I thought she was referring to my little handicap. She saw my face stiffen and hurried to correct herself. "I don't mean an idiot *that* way. You're the smartest person I've ever met, you know that. But you do a lot of idiotic things," she finished quickly. "Look at the time you wired all the speakers at the Hallowe'en dance so that watchamacallit rock group—what's their name?"

"The Siwash Rock," I supplied. "And that was *last* year."

"The Siwash Rock played like crazy but all anybody could hear was the Benedictine monks singing *Gloria in Excelsis Deo* or something."

"The *Bach Mass in B minor*."

"Whatever! And then you went and did exactly the opposite at the school assembly when Mrs. Powell had that bunch of longhairs from Simon Fraser University come and play their string quartet stuff just before Christmas. Sure, Falko, it was funny, but it was dumb too. What if you'd got caught?"

"Didn't get caught," I reminded her.

"And that idiotic prank with the lockers and the tape recorder. Really weird! If they ever find out, you'll be thrown out of Carleton so fast— You know, Falko, you could really *be* somebody if you wanted."

"I already am somebody."

"But nobody really knows you," she yelled. "Not even me, and I know you better than anyone."

"Trouble with you, Cathy," I said as calmly as I could, "is that you go by appearances, by the way things *seem* to be. You judge the whole book just by glancing at the cover."

"And what's *that* supposed to mean?" demanded Cathy. I could see a cold gleam in her eyes.

"Aw, come on, Cathy! You know Schlieff's a creep. Look at what he did yesterday, or the way he picks on people like Manny McGee. I may do

54

dumb stuff but at least I don't cheat or bully people. Face it. The real reason you want to go out with Schlieff is that he's the right kind of guy. He can give you everything I never could— good looks, friends with the in-crowd and all that. I thought you were better than the rest of them, but underneath you're just as bad!" I stood up to go.

"Wait a minute, Falko," said Cathy, and there was a firmness in her voice that I'd never heard before. I sat down again.

"Considering the number of times I've listened to *you* rant and rave, the least you can do is hear me out. If I was really like 'the rest of them,' do you think I'd still be your friend? Do you realize what it's like listening to you when you're in one of your moods? 'Poor little Falko alone against the world.' I didn't want to say anything about this but I'm sick and tired of hearing you complain about school, about teachers, about parents, about *everything!*" She waited for me to say something, but there was a big lump in the back of my throat.

"Falko, *think* about it! Sure, you've got reasons to gripe. But you never do anything positive about your problems. You don't *really* work on your reading the way you should. You don't go out of your way to make friends. You never think about what you're going to do with your life when you're out of school. Your problem is that you're too busy criticizing other people's faults to see your own. You say Henry's a snob, but you're just as bad!"

I was reeling from shock. "Why didn't you ever say any of this before?"

"Oh, come *on!* I tried, Falko. I really did. But you always turned it into a joke or walked away from it."

"What do you want me to do? Pretend everything's wonderful?"

"Of course not!" Cathy seemed a bit calmer now but I was so busy trying not to cry that I hardly noticed. "Falko, all I want you to do is think your problems out more and then do something about them. Whining isn't—"

"All right, already! If you're so sick of me and my problems I'll get out of here before I bore you to death." I didn't mean to sound so bitter and I knew I wasn't being fair, but I had to leave before I broke down. I stood up again.

"You *know* that's not what I meant. I don't want to lose you as a friend—"

"Oh, cut it out, Cathy. I understand. Go ahead and reform Henry. Just don't expect me to help you!" I turned towards the door.

"Wait—"

"Goodbye, Cathy." I didn't wait for an answer. I knew I'd already said too much and the only way to get out of it was to make a clean, dramatic exit.

Outside in the rain I broke into a run to clear my head. This time I'd really screwed things up. For good. And the worst part was the feeling in the back of my head that everything Cathy had said was true.

6.

The next day, Monday, was Day 1 on the school
calendar, which meant we had a reading lab in
English. Harrad loved Day 1. He'd given us a
battery of tests—McGinities and Stanfords and
God knows what else—at the beginning of the
year to determine our "independent and instruc-
tional reading levels." I was diagnosed to be
working on stories at the rose-colour level of the
SRA kit.

I don't know what SRA stands for—since it's
for people like me, probably Simpletons, Retards
and Abnormals! But I do know all about SRA
kits. They're supposed to improve your reading
comprehension by giving you lots of interesting
stories at different levels of difficulty. *Enough
variety to meet the needs of both the gifted and
less able reader,* I think the publicity blurb on
the box says. I've been on them since grade eight.
Being on SRA is like using any addictive drug. If

you're on it long enough you get hooked and eventually get violent withdrawal symptoms if you try to read anything else.

I had been on rose for more than a year. I liked the stories and had all the answers memorized so I could finish my work early and use any extra time for daydreaming or free reading of the *Scope* magazines that littered the room. I also made sure I never scored above seventy percent on the comprehension tests because then I would be promoted to orange. I liked being rose. It seemed a warmer, friendlier colour somehow.

But that morning I couldn't concentrate. First I kept thinking about Cathy, who hadn't shown up for classes. And second there was the little pink administration slip that Harrad had left on my desk with a flourish. It was a summons to the vice-principal's office during lunch hour. I racked my brain trying to figure out what Big Bird wanted to see me for, but I couldn't come up with an answer.

Mr. Frost couldn't have received Wendy's letter from Buffalo yet, so that wasn't it. And anyway, even if he suspected a hoax he had no way of connecting me with it. Must be something else. But what? And then, with a sinking feeling in my guts, I remembered. I hadn't gone to Big Bird's detention on Friday at 3:30! I'd been so busy thinking about Cathy and feeling sorry for myself that I'd forgotten all about it. That meant another bawling out.

"Whatsa matter?"

It was little Ralph Palmer who sat in front of me. He always took an interest in other people's problems.

"Big Bird. I missed his detention on Friday so he wants to see me," I whispered.

Ralph's face registered horror and disbelief. "Better you than me, Falkenheimer. You're *really* out of luck."

"Story of my life," I whispered back. "I got a fortune cookie once that had no fortune in it."

I tried to concentrate on my reading. It was one of my favourite stories, mainly because it was about Houdini. Finally I raised my hand to indicate that I'd finished. One thing they always test you on is your reading time.

"It's 9:16, Albert," said a gentle voice behind me. I turned and saw Miss Baxter, a new student teacher assigned to Harrad. I'd completely forgotten she was sitting at the back of the room. "Did you enjoy your Houdini?" she asked with a smile.

"Yeah," I nodded, smiling too. I liked Miss Baxter. You could tell she wasn't a real teacher because she was friendly and helpful and treated students like human beings.

"Would you mind telling me something about him?"

I gave her the works—not only what was in the story I'd just read, but everything else I knew.

Baxter looked startled. "You're a real Houdini freak, aren't you?"

"I guess so. I like his style. He could escape from anything and he never depended too much on his assistants. In the final crunch it was just himself he relied on."

"Ever tried any of his tricks, Albert?"

"My friends call me Falko. Yeah, a few. But I use more modern equipment, stuff I put together. Houdini died in the twenties so he was sort of limited in what he could do."

Baxter smiled—a real smile, not the condescending "I'm the teacher, you're the dumb kid" smile I was used to. She looked across the room at Harrad and then back at me. "You've got me interested, Falko. How'd you like to write a paper on Houdini? I don't think you'd have to do much research and the paper wouldn't have to be a long one. I'm sure Mr. Harrad would agree to let you do some of the work in class—"

"Uh, okay," I said doubtfully. Was this me, Albert Falkenheimer, volunteering to do extra work? I looked over at Cathy's empty seat and said a silent "So there!" But when Baxter walked away my thoughts turned again to the little pink slip. Who cared if I got along well with student teachers. People like Big Bird were the ones who held my life in their hands.

The bell for lunch finally put me out of my misery and I dragged my feet along to the office. At least there was nobody else waiting. I handed my dog-eared administration slip to the younger secretary, the one who chews gum, and she told me to take a seat on the bench. Some day that bench will be in a museum along with the stuff from the Spanish Inquisition: torture racks, thumb screws and worse.

Five minutes later I was in Big Bird's office looking up at his frowning face. The armchair I was sitting in was so low that my head was barely level with the desk top. Big Bird probably had a chair like that deliberately, just so he could look down on everyone. I was waiting for Sowerby the janitor to pump some fear up through the air vents—the whole school was wired—but for some unknown reason I felt confident.

"You didn't show for detention on Friday, Falkenheimer."

"No, sir."

"Why not?"

I shrugged my shoulders. Big Bird waited grimly.

"Very well, if that's all you have to say for yourself," he said finally, "I have a note here for your parents. I would like to see one or both of them as soon as possible." He handed me an envelope. "And I'll expect to see you in the detention room today at 3:30. You may leave."

I hoisted myself up from the collapsed armchair and got out of there as fast as I could. By then everyone had taken off for lunch so the halls were deserted. I grabbed my lunch bag from my locker and headed for the park across the road from the school, Big Bird's envelope in my hip pocket.

What rotten luck. Now my mother would have to come down to the school. She'd listen to Big Bird and go home and tell my dad. Then I'd really get it.

The only person in sight was Bent William, a

crippled, slightly retarded old guy who was always wandering around the school grounds looking for empty bottles. Sometimes I used to put them all in one place where I knew he would find them. That day he was poking around his favourite spot, the rhododendron bushes outside the schoolyard. I don't know what got into me, but on the spur of the moment I went over to him.

"Mr. William," I hollered at him, "you're wanted. Wanted inside!" I pointed to the school. Bent William swung his head sideways so he was looking up at me, and then he muttered something through his toothless gums. I pointed to the school again and took him by the arm. He allowed himself to be taken up the front steps, through the main door and into the vice-principal's office. I parked him on the bench outside Big Bird's office where he sat uncomprehendingly, his bottle collection bag resting on the floor, his cane held upright between his knees.

I walked around the office desk. The fastest gum-chewer in the West flapped her mouth at me silently, eyes round and questioning.

"Please tell Mr. Bird that my father, Mr. William Falkenheimer, is waiting to see him," I told her as I turned and left the office to take the rest of the day off. For health reasons.

Even though Mom and Dad were at work, I opened the kitchen door quietly. Gran might be sleeping and I didn't want to disturb her.

But she wasn't asleep. "That you home early, Albert?" The singsong tones of her native Yorkshire accent preceded her tiny figure as she pushed herself through the living room door in her wheelchair. She was still in her pink nightdress and her hair hadn't been brushed.

"Hi, Gran." I kissed her lightly on the top of her head. She pushed a rebellious lock of grey hair from her eyes as she smiled up at me over wire-frame spectacles.

"You looked flushed, Albert. Are you coming down with summat?"

I assured her I was fine. "Have you had lunch, Gran? Like me to make you a nice cup of tea? A sandwich?"

"No thanks, luv. I've had tea. I'm fine."

Gran sometimes doesn't look after herself properly, especially when she isn't feeling so good. She has arthritis in her legs and hands. This, combined with her age, her forgetfulness and her generally poor health, serves to make matters even worse. The amount of food she eats wouldn't keep a sparrow alive, to use one of her own expressions. She's lived with us for as long as I can remember. Usually when I say, "Cup of tea, Gran?" her face lights up. She loves her cup of tea.

I'll never forget the afternoon I came home from primary school with a lump over my eye. Some of the kids had been calling me names and I'd got into a fight. Gran wasn't in a wheelchair in those days. She was horrified when she saw the bruise and ran to the kitchen to get a cold compress.

"What happened, luv?" Her face was filled with worry and concern as she pressed the compress gently over my eye.

"Got it fightin'," I answered proudly, "an' I would've won if I hadn't tripped over. Someone kicked me when I was down! That wasn't fair, Gran, was it? Not when I was down."

"Who? Who was fighting?" Gran was angry.

"Bunch of 'em. Jumped me after school."

"Who were they?"

I shrugged. "Just a bunch of kids."

"But why?"

"That's awful cold, Gran. It's so cold it hurts."

"Why do you get into fights, Albert?"

"They—they call me names."

"Like what?"

"I dunno. Like 'stupid.' "

Gran said nothing.

"And 'retard.' Stuff like that."

"You need a thicker towel for the ice. Hold that one there till I get back."

After a while she hadn't come back and the ice pack was making my head ache. So I took it off and went into the kitchen. Gran was standing with her head bowed against the linen-closet door. She was crying.

"Hey, you okay, Gran?" I put my arm around her waist. "Is somethin' wrong?"

She wiped her eyes quickly, impatiently, with the back of her hand and gave a sniff.

"Don't worry 'bout me fightin', Gran. I'm a good fighter. Really I am."

"Here take this towel. Put the ice in it and put it back on your eye. Do as I tell you."

That happened years ago when I was just a kid. Gran was always like a second mother to me. Now that she's in a wheelchair I feel like we're brother and sister. My parents push both of us around and sometimes she gives me the kind of look I imagine fellow prisoners give each other when the warden gets mad. The afternoon I came home early, I decided we both needed to escape.

"Say, Gran, how'd you like me to chauffeur you to the park? It's a beautiful day. Trees smell great. Hawthorns are still in blossom and those Japanese whatchamacallits, the ones with the creampuffs—"

"Snowballs."

"Yeah, and then there's laburnums and I don't know what else. Come on, I'll get your sweater for you."

"You're a good boy, Albert. Just let me go clean up a bit and I'll be right with you."

Later, as I was pushing Gran's wheelchair through the park, she asked me how things were at school.

I said everything was just fine. I didn't want to think about school. We were at the top of a slight hill and to distract Gran's attention from me I decided to take her for a little joyride. By the time we reached the bottom I was having trouble keeping up with the wheelchair, but Gran was giggling like a girl and there was some colour in her cheeks.

As we climbed another hill I wondered what Gran thought about all day long. I couldn't remember ever seeing her reading—not even a newspaper or a magazine. Maybe she didn't know how. Maybe dyslexia ran in the family. She watched TV a lot during the day. In the evening she watched it again but usually fell asleep in the middle of a program.

I knew Mom was worried about the old lady. I heard her tell Dad that she'd soon have to think about quitting work so she could stay home and look after Gran. She was getting forgetful. She might leave the stove on and start a fire or have an accident and be unable to reach the phone. Being old couldn't be much fun. But then being young wasn't much fun either.

*   *   *

As we sat down for supper I pushed Gran's chair into her usual place at the table, facing my own. Mom sat down on Gran's left. "Why, Mother, you have some colour in your cheeks. Whatever have you been doing?"

"Albert took me for a lovely walk—or should I say run?—in the park. Didn't you, luv?" Gran smiled fondly at me.

I coughed with embarrassment and tried to change the subject. "Mom, there's no Rice Krispies left in the cupboard. Why don't you pick up some of those new Flakies, the ones they advertise on—"

"When did you go out?" my inquisitive mother wanted to know.

Gran blew it. "Why, it was just after lunch, wasn't it, dear?"

"Well, I wouldn't—"

"Didn't you go to school this afternoon, Albert?" My mother's voice was stern.

"Wasn't feeling too good. I think I've got malaria."

"Nonsense!"

"Or maybe it's just growing pains. This morning I suddenly got these terrible shooting pains in my knees and elbows. I swear I could feel myself growing! Really! Measure me. I'll bet I've grown two sizes at least! Then I felt it in my wrists and ankles. It shot through—"

"Albert, that's enough. Here's your father."

Dad stared at me, tight-lipped, as he came in and sat down. Nobody said anything while Mom started to serve the food, but my father didn't take his eyes off me. I grabbed the potato dish and helped myself to a couple of B.C.'s best, waiting for somebody to break the silence.

"Well, Albert, what's the story?"

I decided on the light approach. "What story, Pop?"

"The story that Mr. Bird told me. And don't call me Pop." He looked at my mother. "The vice-principal phoned me at work this afternoon. At work yet! It seems that your son here," he nodded at me as he unfolded his napkin, "has been giving Mr. Bird a hard time."

As he launched into an (exaggerated) account of Bent William's effect on Big Bird, my mother bit her lip. "Oh, Albert, how could you? Poor

Bent William! That's simply awful. The poor man isn't in his right mind and you know it." She turned to my father. "He was wounded in the war. Has a piece of shrapnel in his brain, so they say. I'm ashamed of you, Albert. You'll apologize to that poor man even if he doesn't understand you. Who knows? Perhaps he understands more than we think."

Throughout my mother's speech Gran had been nattering away trying to make herself heard. Now her voice broke in, " . . . gas."

"Gas?" asked my mother, her eyes wide with surprise.

"Yes, gas, not shrapnel. That's what I'm sayin'. 'Twasn't shrapnel on the brain. 'Twas gas in his lungs what did it."

My father coughed politely to let the ladies know he was ready to say something just as soon as they got through, but they didn't notice him.

"Well, that's not what *I* heard. In any case, it doesn't change anything. It doesn't alter the fact that—"

"Do you mind?" bellowed my father. When he had silence, he turned to me again. "Well, Albert?" he enquired quietly. "What's the story?"

I shrugged my shoulders. "I'm sorry, Dad. I guess I shouldn't have done it. I'll see Mr. Bird first thing in the morning. I'll apologize. And to Bent William too when I see him again. Okay?"

"Why did you do it, son?"

"I dunno. Just comes over me, I guess. I get fed up with that school sometimes."

There followed a short silence as we all turned our attention to Mom's tuna casserole.

"What's the story about next year?" my father asked, even though he knew I was planning to quit school this summer at the end of grade ten.

"I dunno, Dad. I haven't thought about it yet. Look for a job, I guess."

"Albert, you really *should* be thinking seriously about your Life," Mom exclaimed. Poor Mom! She always worries and she has an earnest way of saying "Life" with a capital L.

"What about the Vocational Institute?" my father asked. "You could take automotive or television repair or something like that. You're good at electronics and the money's good once you get your ticket."

"Yeah, maybe. I've got to think about it," I replied noncommittally.

I didn't really want to go in for anything like that. Another year or two of school? And then a further year or two of work at some dull, routine job before I'd have enough money saved. And saved for what? To escape? To what? It was all too confusing. But one thing I did know was that I wanted to live *now,* not fritter the years away on never-ending five-year plans. Trivia talked like my parents too. Plans! Two years for this, two years for that. Life was always somewhere in the future.

I never liked talking about the future with my parents. They always wanted definite answers and I was afraid I'd explode in their faces if they pushed me too far. The truth was that I hadn't really got along with them for quite a while. When they first found out about my dyslexia they were great—endlessly patient and understanding. But for the last couple of years Dad in particular had been bugging me. "Work harder... Make plans... Ask your guidance counsellor."

Somehow I knew that everything would work out okay. I'd prove to my parents, my guidance counsellors, Cathy—and even Henry Schlieff—that I wasn't a complete loss. There was just one problem. How?

*   *   *

I apologized to Big Bird the next morning and was rewarded with an extra week's detentions. It seemed he wasn't too happy about my joke with Bent William, but he actually paid me a compliment. He said it showed imagination and inventiveness, even though it was in poor taste to involve poor old William in it. And why couldn't I use some of my imagination *in* class instead of out?

Later, as I hurried to pull my books out of my locker, I overheard an interesting conversation.

"Hey, Chuck, how ya doin', man?" Perennial hood Lucio Zanatta threw an arm around the manly shoulders of Henry Schlieff and grinned as though they shared a secret. Henry was apparently trying to change his squeaky-clean image by getting friendly with some of the school's more notorious characters.

70

"Hey, Lucio, whaddya say?" Henry was starting to talk like his new buddies. And "Chuck" seemed to be his new nickname.

"You got the answers for the Socials test?" asked Lucio.

"Sure. Here." Henry handed him a sheet of notepaper as they left their lockers and walked into homeroom.

They both had Mr. Sampson for Socials. Henry's class was in Block B and Lucio's in Block H. Sampson must have given a test in Block B the day before, which meant Block H would get it today. You'd think Mr. Sampson would wise up. Or maybe he knew but, like me, didn't care anymore.

Then I remembered Cathy and realized I did care. I also wondered how much she knew about Schlieff and his friends.

* * *

After homeroom I opened my locker to get some notepaper for Science class.

"Falkenheimer! What are you doing at your locker?"

I jumped with fright. Old Harrad was barking at me—it was a criminal offense to go to your locker between periods. But what did he *think* I was doing at my locker?

The great Houdini stepped into the metal locker. His hands were chained together at the wrists. The door was closed and the lock snapped into place. How could anyone escape from such a prison? But nothing and nobody had ever held Houdini against his will. Three minutes later the lock was unfastened and the door thrown open. Houdini had disappeared. Flown away. A mocking laugh filled the crowded hall and then faded away, its faint echoes reverberating in the stillness.

"Are you all right, Falkenheimer?" asked Harrad, pushing his horror movie mask into my white face.

I recoiled in horror. "Y-yessir!"

"Take twenty-five lines for being at your locker without permission!"

"Th-thank you, sir!" I retreated from him, walking backwards slowly. He watched me for a moment, a frown furrowing his forehead, and then turned on his heel and marched off.

How was I going to show the world I was a somebody if I couldn't even get away with opening my locker?

7.

"Hello, Falko. How are you?"

"Hi, Cathy. I'm fine. And you?"

"Fine."

Awkward pause.

"How's the Annual going?"

"Oh, that was all finished ages ago."

Another awkward pause.

"You going down to the cafeteria for lunch?"

"Sure. You?"

"Yeah. Let's eat. So what's the latest from the Grad Committee?"

"Oh, not much. We can't decide what should be done with the hundred and twenty-five dollars we made on the sock hop. You know the school Eagle was stolen?"

"Yeah."

"Well, maybe we'll buy a new one for the main hall."

We finally found a table in the cafeteria. "How come you haven't phoned or been over to the house?" asked Cathy.

"Didn't think you wanted me to."

"But I said I still meant for us to be friends. I-I've missed talking with you, Falko."

"What about Henry?"

"Well, we're friends too. But you're my *best* friend. At least I want it to be that way. If it's okay with you."

"Sure it is, Cathy. I'm stupid. We don't own each other. I've missed talking too. And I'm sorry about some of the things I said. I know they weren't true."

"So we're friends again?"

"Of course. Come over to my place after supper, okay?"

"I'd like that." She smiled.

Outside, the sun climbed towards the top of the sky.

"You finished? Let's take a walk in the park before the bell rings."

Cathy laughed like old times. "Let's!"

After almost three weeks of not talking to each other, that's how Cathy and I became friends again.

* * *

The temperature in Harrad's room was ninety-eight below, so cold that even sound froze. Big John Whitelaw, a good-natured seventeen-year-old with a dull expression, sat behind me at the back of the class with his feet propped up on the lower rungs of Schlieff's and my desks, and I was feeling the pressure from behind. When he accidentally shoved our desks forward with his feet the resulting sound—a long, groaning scrape in the stillness—assailed the air like the sharp crack of an ice-floe splitting.

Harrad, sitting behind his desk with the refrigeration machine on maximum power, looked up quickly, saw Whitelaw's size thirteen barges shifting to the floor and fixed him with a look of hatred. And then Siberian silence again.

The whole class was getting restless. We had less than a month of school left now and already people were thinking about summer. In Harrad's class, though, my fingers were still frostbitten. They were so numb that I could hardly feel the pages of *Teenage Tales* as I turned them.

Read the second story of the book. Answer the vocabulary questions at the back of the book. Then do the 'Check Your Understanding' questions. Neatly, in your workbooks. There will be no talking. Help, I'm lost in the frozen tundra! Only one match left to light a fire, my frostbitten fingers unable to feel the matchbox or the match. If this one sputters out I'm raw meat.

Each story was about half a dozen pages in length. It took me a long time to read that much, especially when the print was small. I was supposed to be writing down the answers to the questions, but my brain was as frostbitten as my fingers.

Over by the door, Charlene Jamieson was weeping.

Charlene was a big, shapeless girl with fuzzy,

light-brown hair and a face that wore a permanent air of distraction and worry. The other kids made fun of her attempts to make herself important, but I felt sorry for her. About two weeks earlier, on one of her flights of fantasy, Charlene had told several people that her boyfriend had one week to live. Nobody believed she had a boyfriend, let alone a dying one.

Just before class had begun, Rick Symes, the class clown, had asked in a loud voice, "Hey, Charlene, how's your boyfriend? Isn't he dead yet?"

The other kids thought Charlene's angry reaction was hysterical. "Leave her alone," I said, rooting for the underdog as usual.

Cathy chimed in, "Yes, don't be so mean!"

"Well, when he dies, Falko will have you, Charlene!" Symes' face was red with laughter.

Then everybody shut up, leaving Charlene alone with her humiliation.

Now Harrad finally noticed her weeping. "Is there something wrong?" Voice emotionless, hard, critical. Like one of those expressionless plastic dolls with the cord in the back. Pull the cord, release, doll talks: "Baby sleepy."

Charlene didn't answer, just jumped to her feet and ran from the room.

Harrad shook his head in annoyance and another blast of biting Arctic air raised goosebumps under my summer shirt.

"Eighteen days of school left," I reminded myself. "Eighteen days."

* * *

"Mrs. Powell! Mrs. Powell!"

Mr. Frost came flapping into our Music class waving a sheet of paper in one hand and an envelope in the other. It looked as if the New York letter had arrived at last!

"Could you step outside for a moment, Mrs. Powell?" requested the principal. She followed him into the hallway and closed the door behind her.

I felt funny—sort of elated that my trick was working, a little scared in case something went wrong, and unsure of a tiny nagging feeling that I couldn't quite define.

When Mrs. Powell came back into the classroom her face was pale. She was holding the letterhead I'd forged with Trivia's assistance and she seemed distracted and worried. I was beginning to wish I hadn't done it. Then I remembered how she'd made me look like a fool in front of all those kids, many of whom were only grade eights and nines. She deserved to stew for a while!

* * *

I was trying to listen to Cathy's bright chatter but I couldn't stop thinking about Powell and Frost. I'd managed to clarify my feelings about the fake copyright letter and now I wished I hadn't done it.

I imagined both Powell and Frost reading the letter, imagined their horror on learning they were to be sued for using copyrighted music material without permission. They must be worried, thinking of the adverse publicity for the school, of the scandal, of the possible financial hardship. I'd thought I would feel good about it, but instead I was developing a bad case of guilt. What a letdown! After all, by now they might have discovered the hoax and were just mad that someone had tried to sabotage the school production.

I tried to tell Cathy all about it but the words stuck in my throat. For her part, she knew something was wrong. I could tell by the kind of frantic way she kept on talking.

"Sometimes I think you've got the right attitude to school," she complained as she pushed her hair back from her face. A capricious offshore breeze tempered the afternoon heat as we strolled along the sea wall at Third Beach. "I mean, what a bore! Thursday I've got to have a Socials report for Sampson and I haven't even started it yet."

I grinned at her unsympathetically. "What is it? One of his famous two-hundred-page monstrosities on the mating habits of Mongolian banjo players?"

"Very funny! But you're not too far off. It's twenty pages. Japan—physical features, industrial growth. Usual stuff. Seems like I've been spending most of my young life writing Socials reports."

"Come on, let's find ourselves a big flat log to lean against down on the beach." I pulled Cathy with me as I leapt over the sea wall and onto the sand. I was running so fast that she had trouble hanging on to the shoulder strap of her guitar case as we sped down the beach. Finally we collapsed in a tangled heap on the leeward side of a long horizontal fir, its barkless trunk worn smooth by wind, rain and sand. We lay panting for a while in exaggerated postures of exhaustion. I let my senses drink in the rolling sound of the surf, the cries of the gulls, the healing smell of the sea and the rich gold-yellow of the day. And then I reached for Cathy's hand.

"When you get your breath back will you play for me?"

Cathy smiled, took her guitar from its case and began to tune up. Her face grew serious as her fingers found the chords and she began to sing.

When she finished there was no need to say anything. She lay down, her head next to mine, eyes closed against the brightness of the sun. Her long lashes curved to reflect the afternoon light, and a delicate curling smile brushed the corners of her lips.

A seagull screeched somewhere overhead as it rode the winds between the mountains and the shore. "This is perfection," I thought. Powell and Frost and my guilt all melted away.

Slowly, tentatively, I put my hand on Cathy's shoulder.

"Cathy ... "

Her eyes opened and met mine. And then she said very quietly and gently, "Just friends, Falko, remember?"

"Just friends."

*　*　*

For the first time in weeks Cathy called me early on a Saturday morning.

"You got anything planned, Falko? I thought we might go for a swim or something."

"No, nothing planned except a big breakfast *soon*. I'd love a swim. Which beach shall we grace with our perfect bodies?"

"Why don't we take a picnic lunch," suggested Cathy, "and go to Lynn Canyon for a change? We could take a bus."

It didn't take me long to agree. Lynn Canyon is a really nice spot in the North Shore mountains—trees, trails, deep freshwater pools along the length of the creek and a narrow suspension bridge over the gorge.

"Good idea. I'll pick you up in an hour or so."

When I got to Cathy's place she wasn't quite ready, so Mrs. Robinson asked me in. I told her I'd just sit in the back yard and enjoy the sunshine.

As soon as I'd settled down into a lounge chair Mrs. Robinson came out and pretended to adjust the clothesline. I wondered why she wanted to talk to me. The only time she ever acted friendly was when something was about to go wrong.

"You're up early, Albert. Didn't you go to the party last night?"

"No, I stayed home." What party? I hadn't heard about any party.

There was a pause just long enough to make me feel uncomfortable.

80

"Do you know a boy named Henry Schlieff?"

"Sure." So *that* was it.

"What kind of boy is he?"

I didn't know what Cathy had told her so I decided to play dumb. "He's okay, I guess. Don't know much about him."

"Well, I don't think he's much of a gentleman," said Mrs. Robinson. "He called for Cathy at eight o'clock and Mr. Robinson told him to be sure and have her home by eleven. She finally arrived home—on her own—at almost midnight. That young man hasn't heard the last of this yet, not by a long shot."

I smiled to myself. Maybe Mrs. Robinson wasn't as bad as I'd made her out to be.

Just then Cathy came out onto the back porch. "Mother, Falko doesn't want to hear about that. Come on, Falko, let's go."

By now I was getting curious, so on the way to the bus stop I asked, "What was all that about?"

"Oh, nothing," answered Cathy. "I'll tell you about it later. What have you brought to eat in that packsack of yours? I've got some delicious codfish eyeballs and an octopus tentacle marinated in marzipan sauce."

"Well, I can't beat that," I said, grinning. "But I *have* brought a jar of pickled pigsfeet and some—"

"Ugh! I've never tasted pigsfeet," Cathy shuddered.

"Wait, let me finish. Then I've got some left-over Lithuanian lambs' livers wrapped in limp lettuce leaves, and a whole chunk of Katenwurst made from selected homeless German alleycats."

Cathy pretended to throw up her breakfast so realistically that a passing lady stopped to stare with distaste.

"Do you realize," Cathy said when we'd found seats on the bus, "that it's only two weeks away from the grad party and then we're finished at Carleton High?"

"Yeah, I know," I grinned at her happily. "You looking forward to Benson?" Benson is the senior high school.

"Sure, but I'll miss you, Falko. Have you decided what you're going to do?"

"Yes, I'm going on safari. To the Amazon. I'm going to try and find the lost tribe of Plango headhunters."

"And when you find them?"

"I'll introduce them to the benefits of civilization. I'll have sixty native bearers with cases of Coca-Cola to distribute to the chief and his wives. Then I'll erect a huge Coca-Cola sign over the chief's hut. After that I'll try to sell him a McDonald's franchise."

"Do headhunters eat all-beef patties, special sauce, et cetera, on a sesame seed bun?"

"Not yet but they will. They have to be educated. But seriously, Cathy, just because I'm dropping out shouldn't make any difference. I'll still be around. I'll probably get a job pumping gas or something." She didn't say anything but she smiled and put her hand in mine, and I knew she understood what I was trying to say.

Later we made our way unsteadily over the scary swinging bridge that spanned the gorge. Far below us the waters rushed and tumbled over jagged rocks. We stopped in the middle of the bridge to look down. Cathy made a ladylike spit over the side and I imitated her. We watched the tiny white blobs curve and float down to be lost in the foaming waters below.

"Hey," I grinned. "With talent like that I could use you on my expedition!"

We followed a trail through mossy cliffs and tall firs to the swimming hole, a deep pool surrounded by the walls of the canyon. The ice-cold water was moving and swirling on the surface, and the sound of a waterfall could be heard echoing through a cleft in the rocks.

After our swim we spread ourselves out on the great smooth rocks to dry off, and lay there in silence as our frozen bodies began to soak up the warm sunshine.

"So, what's all this about Henry?" I asked.

"You mean last night?"

I nodded at her as I began opening my packsack in search of food. The swim had made me hungry.

"There's not much to tell," she said. "Henry asked me out to a 'coketail' party at Mark Sondquist's house. He picked me up in his dad's car and we got there about eight-fifteen. The place was crowded—mostly Benson High kids as far as I could see. Well, they were drinking Coke all right, but they were mixing it with other stuff —gin, vodka, rum. And a few of the kids were smoking dope. The record player was on real loud and a bunch of kids were dancing and necking. Henry was drinking hard stuff with that guy Lucio and he wanted me to have some too, but I said no.

"Around half past ten I wanted to go home. I wasn't enjoying myself anyway, but I didn't say anything to Henry because he seemed to be having a good time. He obviously didn't want to leave and when I reminded him that I had to be home by eleven, he said, 'Just one more for the road.' He was already a little drunk and on top of that he'd been smoking with Mark and Lucio. He was giggling and talking a lot of nonsense, and I began to worry about him driving. When eleven o'clock came and Henry was still drinking it up with his friends I figured he'd forgotten all about me, so I left and walked home."

"I *told* you Henry was a creep."

"But Falko, you don't understand. Henry's a bit weak, yes, but he's not like those others. I've got to help him."

I couldn't believe my ears. Help Henry? "How do you mean, help him?"

"Help him get away from that bunch of freaks."

"How do you intend to do that?"

"I don't know yet but I'll think of something."

Poor Cathy. Doing her salvation thing. I read

somewhere that women love to reform men. I'll never understand it. Anyway, I didn't want to get into an argument so I let the whole thing drop.

"Well, while you're figuring out a way to get Henry on the side of the angels, I'm going to enjoy some of your chicken." I plunged my hand into her picnic lunch and kept my thoughts to myself. I knew what I'd do with Henry! I'd have him shot at dawn every day for a month. Letting her walk home alone at midnight. And taking a girl like Cathy to that rat's nest in the first place. What a creep! But now that we were just friends, I didn't feel I could tell Cathy how to run her life.

It was the biggest mistake I ever made.

8.

I was sitting in my hard, uncomfortable desk in Science class plotting revenge on Henry Schlieff. Parker had been off sick for weeks with some mysterious ailment. The substitute, a young guy with long hair and a beard, was doing his best to control the class and be nice at the same time. Substitutes usually try hard to be good guys, so naturally the kids take advantage of what they see as a weakness in the enemy defenses. They act like a bunch of crazies.

Right now there seemed to be a concerted attack on John Whitelaw. He was sitting as usual, his normally pleasant face a little puzzled at the attention he was attracting from some of the other kids. Every time the teacher turned to write on the blackboard, paper darts and spitballs showered down on John. The sub, unaware of what was going on behind his back, kept writing merrily away until he heard Louise Potter giggle. Then he frowned and turned around to face the class.

"Is there something wrong?"

Nobody answered. He just grinned and turned back to the blackboard, his voice racing along in an explanation of an equation that Parker had taught us months before. Needless to say, no one had told him we already knew it. We were all having too much fun.

Things began to heat up when little Tony Singleton fired a spitball at Janice Ferster. Janice tried to turn around to face her assailant, but all she could move was her head. Out of the corner of her eye she could see Tony preparing another spitball.

"Cut it out, Tony," she whispered in a hoarse voice.

Just then Tony let his second spitball fly from the rubber band between his fingers. It hit Charlene Jamieson, who sat near the door, right on the side of her face. Charlene whirled around and saw Tony's rubber band and his mocking grin. She jumped from her seat, lunged over to grab Tony's rubber band and screamed in a paroxysm of fury, "Gimme that!"

Meanwhile the poor sub had faced the class again, his face pale, and demanded to know what was going on.

By now Janice had joined the attack on Tony. While Charlene held him by the wrist and tried to get the rubber band, Janice grabbed his hair in her huge fist and pulled him screaming to the floor. The rest of the class added their voices to the confusion and soon the room was bedlam.

The sub raced around the edge of the battle zone but he didn't know how to handle the situation. The class was completely out of control. Louise's giggling had become hysterical and several desks had toppled over as Janice and Charlene, shouting and punching, tried to destroy Tony Singleton once and for all.

The only one unaffected by the confusion was John Whitelaw, who sat staring at the mayhem with a blank expression of disbelief.

Just then the classroom door was thrown violently open. Big Bird to the rescue! He strode to the front of the room, rested his hands on his hips and roared, "Enough!" All it took was that one word. The bodies began to separate themselves. The spectators had slid back into their seats at the first sight of the vice-principal, and now Janice, Charlene and Tony put their desks upright and sat down, their faces flushed with the excitement of battle.

Big Bird's face was contorted with anger as he stood like Zeus about to fire his powerful thunderbolts at the Titans. "You three people report to my office at 3:15 sharp." He looked like he was trying hard to control an urge to rip them apart with his bare hands. The room was so quiet I could hear the buzz of a bluebottle throwing itself against the window.

Bird turned and looked at the helpless sub, then at the class. "I shall leave the door open. If I hear so much as a whisper from this room for the rest of the period I'll be back. Count on it!"

He gave the sub one last withering look and marched from the room, trailing silence in his wake.

Things settled down to near-Parker normal except that nobody bothered to do any work. I returned to my musing on Henry Schlieff. What kind of revenge would suit his crime?

Suddenly a picture of Charles Bronson in *The Mechanic* flashed into my mind. Wow, what a movie! Bronson was a hit man, an expert killer— cold, emotionless, a real perfectionist.

Henry Schlieff, opening his locker, didn't notice the Falcon disguised as a maintenance man repairing the thermostat just inside the doorway of Room 26. The repairman pressed a button on the end of his screwdriver and took several pictures of Henry at his locker.

Later, Henry Schlieff jumped on his bicycle and rode through a crowd of kids in the schoolyard. He leaned over the racing handlebars and applied pressure to the brake to slow down at the junction outside the school. There were no other kids in sight. He was alone now. A telephone repairman, stationed in his truck, took several pictures of Henry with the aid of a telephoto lens.

The next day the Falcon, dressed in a silk lounge jacket and ascot tie, paced his luxurious New York apartment, a cigarette and a scotch and water in his left hand. His right hand rested in the pocket of his jacket. Even though he appeared to be perfectly relaxed there was some-

thing about the way he held himself that gave the impression of a coiled steel spring that could snap into action in a micro second.

He strode over to a corkboard wall and switched on a small wall light which illuminated the photographs tacked up beneath it. One showed Henry Schlieff opening his locker, and beside it was an enlargement of Schlieff's hand on the lock. Another picture showed Schlieff riding his ten-speed bicycle. Beside it was an enlargement of his hand on the brake.

The Falcon studied the pictures carefully. Then he removed one photograph and studied it more closely for a few seconds. His mind made up, he gave a piratical grin and flicked the photograph with the nail of his thumb . . .

Two days later, at Vancouver Police Headquarters, the Superintendent's finger stabbed the intercom button. "Send the Chief Inspector in here," he snarled.

The Chief Inspector slid into the room. "Yes, sir." He noticed the worried look on the face of the Superintendent.

"Chief, the Falcon's back in Vancouver. This time it's homicide."

The Chief's face paled under its English Bay tan. "That—that doesn't sound like the Falcon's usual MO," he stuttered.

"It's him all right. Here's his card." The Superintendent handed the Chief Inspector a card bearing a crudely drawn falcon. "It was found in

the victim's pocket."

"How'd it happen, sir?"

"Far as we can tell at this point, a bomb was taped under the saddle of a racing bike belonging to one Henry Schlieff, a student at Carleton High."

"Not the same place as the locker incident?"

"The same," sighed the Superintendent. "Schlieff was riding his bike home from school this afternoon. He pulled the brake handle and blew himself up."

"Dead?" enquired the Chief Inspector.

"What do you think?" snarled the Superintendent. "How would you be if a hunk of gelignite went off under your ass?"

The Chief Inspector thought about that for a few seconds and then shook his head. "Want me to get on it, sir?"

"Get on it, Chief Inspector."

When the Chief had left, the Superintendent leaned back in his swivel chair. His eyes grew misty as he gazed longingly at the photograph of his retirement cottage on Bowen Island.

The third-period bell woke me from my daydream. All the other kids had left and Parker's sub was cleaning off the board. He had a look of defeat about him. I walked up to him and watched the chalk dust settle in his beard. I wanted to say something to him but I didn't know what.

He looked at me nervously. "Yes?" His voice was low and polite.

"Uh—nothing." I turned and left the room. After all, what teacher would listen to the advice of a grade-ten failure?

* * *

That day we all had to sign up for "FED"—Field Experience Day. Some of the kids felt it should be called Fed-up Day, but one good thing about it was that it meant we spent a day in June outside instead of frying in the Carleton grease pits. FED was the brainchild of Big Bird. Get the little bounders outside, eh what? Trivia always said Bird should have been a scoutmaster instead of a vice-principal.

We had our choice of a trip to Stanley Park, one to the sugar refinery, another to a linen supply company, a couple to Simon Fraser University and one to Gastown. I wasn't really interested in any of them, having been to most of them before at one time or another, but I had to make a choice or Big Bird would lay an egg.

It was raining, but Trivia arrived on time. "Made your choice, Falko?" His eyes blinked behind his huge spectacles.

"Not really."

"What about Burke Mountain?"

"I didn't know it was being offered."

"Yeah, they added it on Friday. Parker's sub is taking it."

When I think of that teacher, I wonder if he had a name of his own. I can't remember him ever being called anything but Parker's sub. Maybe it *was* his real name. Anyway, if he was supervising the trip to Burke Mountain it meant we could do pretty well whatever we wanted.

Nearing the school we caught sight of the line-up. Big Bird's Pillsbury Doughboy head could be seen bobbing up and down, maintaining law and order.

We parked ourselves behind the bulk of Janice Ferster, who was babbling away to a pimple-faced grade-eight girl, trying to persuade her to go to the sugar refinery. "They give samples!" Janice needed sugar samples like the Sahara needs sand.

Further up the line I could hear the nasal ego-tones of Henry Schlieff trying to impress Madeleine Armstrong. Cathy was with them.

The line was getting longer. Linda Holt fell in behind Trivia. "How's it going, Chief?" Linda called everyone Chief. She turned to me. "Going up the mountain, Falko?"

"Yeah, Trivia talked me into it."

"No kidding. Who's taking it?"

"Parker's sub."

"Anyone else?"

"Dunno. Probably some of the student teachers."

The gym was chaos. Big Bird was flapping like one of those gooney birds that take off into the Pacific. The horde swept him out of the way and the Burke Mountain trip was full in ten minutes. Trivia and I just made the cutoff. I saw Schlieff's name—number one, of course—on the sign-up sheet. Maybe we should have gone to the sugar refinery.

* * *

When FED day came it was raining. We milled around in the pre-dawn. I avoided Schlieff, who was holding court at the school entrance while Cathy looked on with an expression that I hoped wasn't admiration.

A strike at the sugar refinery had added Janice Ferster to the Burke Mountain hike. Her massive bulk, resplendent in a yellow slicker, would have been enough to intimidate any hostile picketer. She sneaked a smoke over by the sickly grove of poplars at the north corner of the schoolyard. Two grade eights looked on enviously at her sophistication.

"When's the bus coming?" someone asked.

"Who cares?"

The knot of kids around Schlieff was growing larger. The king and his court. He could have them. It was his queen I grudged him.

"You guys set? How's it going, Chief?" It was Linda Holt, looking like something out of *The Call of the Wild*—hunting shirt, woollen toque, orange packsack and the latest paperback. "I'm really looking forward to this hike."

"Pity about the rain," I replied, hiding my admiration of her cheerful self-confidence.

"Cheer up, Chief, it can't be any worse than school. Hey, there's the bus!"

"Okay, kids, line up!" yelled Parker's sub, who had materialized from one of the school entrances. He looked as nervous and eager to please as ever.

There was a rush as the bus doors creaked open. This bus, from Blue Jay Transport, had obviously seen better days. Schlieff and company moved forward in a solid formation and headed straight for the back. A couple of grade eight kids who beat them to it got bounced up front.

"Three to a seat," shouted Parker's sub.

Linda squeezed in beside Trivia and me. Janice Ferster flattened her two grade-eight admirers as she performed the impossible. Janice by herself was three to a seat.

We were in luck. The only supervisory help Parker's sub had were three student teachers who looked just as harmless as him.

We were told we should be arriving at the foot of Burke Mountain in about thirty minutes. Janice Ferster had started to eat. Linda Holt was reading. Behind us the king could be heard telling his coterie of lapdogs and lackeys one of his tall tales. I glanced back and saw that he had planted himself between Cathy and Madeleine.

Trivia was playing his usual geographical game. He'd coerced Jason Holnyk into it. I gave up playing that game when Trivia exhausted my supply of X's. I mean, apart from Xingu River, Xeres and a few possible Greek ones, how many are there? Poor old Holnyk had fallen for the trap. He said Pugwash, which gave Trivia H, so Trivia said Halifax, which meant Holnyk was left with X. Game over!

When we arrived, Schlieff and company waited haughtily while the bus disgorged the grade eights. Madeleine was laughing at something that Schlieff had said about Janice Ferster's girth.

Burke Mountain is a long, slow climb. Parker's sub was leading, but apparently not fast enough for some.

"C'mon Chief! Time's a-wasting." Linda Holt was obviously on the move and anxious to get to the top. I hung back waiting for Trivia to catch up. I didn't want my poor Hong Kong tire treads competing with Linda's superior Hungarian freedom fighter boots all the way up Burke. She saw me hanging back, so she passed me at a speed I figured could be equalled only by a cheetah with an overdose of Ex-lax. "So long, Chief, see you at the top!" And she was gone.

The line of hikers was spreading out farther and farther. Some of the girls, despite warnings from Parker's sub, had the wrong kind of footwear. One of them had already lost the heel of one of her boots and was hopping along like a Model A pogo stick. One of the student teachers, Miss Scavington, began to puff and wheeze until it looked as if her company on the hike would be limited.

Burke Mountain trail is a killer. It doesn't look that way, but then killers seldom do. The trail is a gradual climb—ever so gradual—like taking a low hill in the first gear of a ten-speed.

"Okay, who was Tom Mix's horse?" It was Trivia's usual kind of question. I was about to say Gene Autry but remembered in time that Trivia took his "camp quizzes" too seriously for me to joke about them. Besides, he'd probably respond by asking me the name of Gene's horse.

We were now about halfway up the trail and the hikers looked like something out of the Klondike gold rush. Although we'd been ordered by Parker's sub not to litter the sides of the trail, it bore the trademarks of all the soft drink and candy bar czars. Janice Ferster had been busy.

The rain, which had almost stopped at the base of the mountain, started coming down harder, and with it a heavy mist. A number of the kids stopped and looked longingly back down the trail. The red-faced Scavington was with them.

"Seen Cathy yet?" asked Trivia.

"No. She must be up ahead."

Through the mist I caught a glimpse of a red toque bobbing at what looked like the front of the line. Linda Holt had obviously made it. Then we saw the kids up ahead turning back.

"What's happening?"

"Parker's sub has ordered a turn-back."

"Why, whatsamatter?"

"Says it's too dangerous in this weather. Get lost in the fog. Besides, we're way behind schedule."

Most of the kids looked only too happy at this

state of affairs. None of us had the proper clothing for hiking in the rain, and after marching for almost an hour we were all pretty soaked and bedraggled. Trivia was worried about getting his nostalgia quiz book wet, while others were beefing about their soaking feet and lunches.

Going back down the trail proved to be no easy task. It was slippery and uncertain. There was a loud bellow from down below as what appeared to be a runaway moonball flattened a couple of hikers with deadly accuracy. It was Janice Ferster. She'd slipped on a candy bar wrapper.

About a half-hour later we found ourselves glumly chewing our sodden sandwiches under the leaking umbrella of a giant cedar.

"What's the name of Hopalong Cassidy's horse?"

"Mae West."

"Don't be so smart, Falko." Trivia sulked in injured silence for a few minutes and then asked the question that had been on my mind. "I wonder where Cathy got to?"

I didn't answer. I was too busy trying to remember when I'd last seen her.

Parker's sub somehow made it back to the bus before Trivia and me, and when we got there he was already shepherding his flock into the dry interior. The kids were jamming the doors to get out of the rain. The student teachers, Scavington in particular, seemed to be too out of it to control all the pushing and shoving. The bus driver, though, was getting impatient. He kept telling

Parker's sub about his deadline to pick up other schools and how he wanted to get moving.

"They all here?" he grumbled.

"I'll get a head count," said Parker's sub. "Would you take it, Miss Scavington, while I check up the trail for any stragglers?"

"Don't be too long," the bus driver shouted at his departing back. "We haven't got all day."

Some of the grade eights began to sing. Janice Ferster consoled herself with a squashed Ding-Dong. Before Scavington could get a count Parker's sub was back.

"No sign of anybody on the trail. Have you made a count?"

"Everybody seems to be here," said Scavington vaguely, only too happy to sit down again and ignore the jeers and shouts of her charges.

"Okay, let's go," muttered the driver. "I've got a schedule to keep."

Cathy was sitting at the back of the bus with one of the girls who worked on the Annual. I couldn't see Schlieff or his stooge, Nicky Benson. Nor could I see Madeleine Armstrong.

I shot a glance around the bus.

"Hey Trivia, did you see Linda Holt coming down?" I asked. Trivia had just given Appomattox to Jason Holnyk and was watching him squirm.

"No. She was up ahead, I think."

I looked back at Cathy. "Where's Schlieff?" I mimed. Cathy signalled for me to shut up and I decided to find out why. The teachers were too zonked to say anything as I slipped down the aisle to her.

"Where's Schlieff?"

Cathy looked worried.

"He took off with Nicky. They said they were going to cross over the back of the mountain. Lucio Zanatta and Mark Sondquist are waiting for them with a car and some 'refreshments.' Henry said he couldn't hack the bus trip back. You know how he hates being with grade eights."

"He's crazy," I whispered. "He'll never make it in this weather. You can hardly see a thing up there."

"I know." Cathy frowned. "Henry wanted me to go along with them but I said I couldn't make it in my heels. Madeleine went though."

"Did you see Linda Holt?"

"She's the Junior Forest Ranger, isn't she? Yeah, she's with them. Henry didn't want her along but she went anyway."

"Look, Cathy, we'd better tell Parker's sub that four people are missing. He's in charge and . . . " I stopped. What was I saying? Parker's sub was a teacher. All teachers, subs or not, were the enemy. I could just see the headlines: *Parker's sub given lifetime detention for losing four Carleton High students*. It didn't seem funny.

"Stop the bus! There are some kids missing," I shouted. Maybe I was doing it for Linda's sake.

Miss Scavington awakened with a start.

I rushed up to Parker's sub. "Four kids are up there. You've got to go back." Parker's sub looked terrified, but he managed to move up towards the driver.

The driver wanted no part of it.

"I got a schedule, mister. You can phone for somebody when you get back to the school."

"Don't worry about it, Bill," Miss Scavington reassured Parker's sub. "They'll probably hitchhike back." By now he looked sick.

Half an hour later we were at the school. The bus emptied and Parker's sub headed straight for the office to huddle with Big Bird. Trivia and Holnyk left without me so I waited for Cathy, who looked as if she needed cheering up.

"They'll be okay. Schlieff has pretty good self-preservation instincts." But Cathy still looked worried.

A screech of tires announced the arrival of Lucio and company.

"Hey, Cath," he shouted. "Where's Chuck?"

Cathy's face paled. "I thought you were picking him up!"

"We waited but he never showed." Lucio scratched his head. "I guess he'll thumb it. See ya!" Another squeal of tires and he was gone.

Cathy was crying. "I shouldn't have let Madeleine go with them. I should have told Parker's sub."

"Take it easy, Cathy. Lean on me. C'mon, let's go to the office and see what Parker's sub is doing."

We arrived in time to see Big Bird at his battle station. "Phone the RCMP, Miss Phelps, and see if they can get a search party for the mountain. I'll phone the parents. What do you want, Falkenheimer?"

"He's the one who told me they were missing, sir," said Parker's sub, who appeared to be barely treading water in the waves Big Bird was setting off.

"Over here, boy! Okay, you were in on this. Speak up!"

"No, he wasn't!" Cathy blurted out. "It was my fault. I knew Henry and Nicky were going to skip out. I could've stopped them but I didn't. It's *my* fault."

Big Bird calmed down. "Very well, let's get the names and all you know about it, Cathy. We'll discuss guilt later. You can stay too, Falkenheimer. Maybe you can help out."

The RCMP arrived and Cathy told them what she knew. After sitting around for an hour waiting for news I walked her home. She was too worried to say much.

"They're probably on their way home right now," I said in a futile attempt to comfort her.

But they weren't on their way home. Or at least they didn't arrive that night. On the late night news the anchorman read a bulletin while the TV camera showed a rescue helicopter taking off over Burke Mountain.

Four high-school students, two boys and two girls, are missing after a school field-trip this afternoon on Burke Mountain, Coquitlam. The four teenagers were separated from a group of

*Carleton High School students when bad
weather conditions resulted in extremely poor vis-
ibility. Names have not been released at this
time. Rescue teams have been combing the rug-
ged mountain area all evening. The search will
continue tomorrow morning.*

*This is the third Burke Mountain incident this
year. Last February the bodies of a couple from
Burnaby—both veteran hikers—were found in the
heavily forested area of the south slope after
being missing for twelve days. And only last
month . . .*

My heart sank. I hoped Cathy wasn't watching.

* * *

The next morning at school was the slowest one
of my life.

Finally, just before lunch hour, the PA an-
nouncement came from Big Bird. The four students lost on FED had been found! They were
tired, wet and hungry but otherwise in good
shape. They would be back at school tomorrow. I
felt a tremendous relief.

The bell rang and I ran out into the hall to
find Cathy. She rushed over to me, a smile on her
face.

"I'm glad they were found, Cathy. Even
though I hate Schlieff's guts, I'm glad he's okay."
We sort of bumped against each other in the
crowded hall. "Come over to the park with your
lunch and we'll have a talk. Okay?"

103

Cathy nodded. "I'll just put my books away and be right with you."

That night the newscast included a big feature on the rescue. A film clip showed a pretty dishevelled group. Schlieff looked like a complete wreck, which was too bad since this was his big chance to be a star. Only Linda Holt looked calm and unruffled. The head of the rescue team gave her all the credit for getting the group down safely.

I sat glued to the set. If Schlieff could get three innocent kids involved in this kind of mess, what was to stop him from doing the same thing to Cathy?

9.

Somebody had finked.

I spent half an hour on the hotseat in Mr. Frost's office. He'd somehow discovered it was me who wrote the copyright letter about the school musical production.

"I sent for you more in sorrow than in anger, Falkenheimer. Why did you do it?" asked the principal, leaning over his desk at me.

I shrugged. "I dunno, sir."

"Do you think it was funny, this practical joke of yours?"

I said nothing.

"Very well, I'm going to have the whole matter passed on to Mr. Bird. I shall let him determine the proper disciplinary measures to be taken. Just let me say this, Falkenheimer, before you go. Practical jokes can sometimes cause unnecessary trouble, or hurt, or suffering. Practical jokes sometimes turn into cruel jokes." He paused, looking at me over his spectacles. When I still said nothing he waved a hand at me. "You may leave."

Later I grilled Trivia. He was the only one who had known. It turned out after heavy cross-examination, that he'd "mentioned" the hoax to Doris. And Doris let a few words slip to Tricia Mack, her best friend. And so on. Somebody—I never found out who—finked.

So I was sitting in my usual place on the bench waiting for Big Bird to see me. I felt as if I'd been through it all before, mainly because I had. Kirby What's-his-name was there beside me; the secretary was chewing gum in that slow vacant way of hers; and the office clock was ticking away the minutes. A numbness began to steal over me, starting with my feet and moving up. But just as the creeping paralysis reached my chin and lower teeth Big Bird's Pillsbury Doughboy face emerged from its office, followed by his Pillsbury Doughboy body.

Big Bird dismissed Kirby with a quick scribble on an administration slip. "Back to class, boy. I'll see you tomorrow."

He turned to me. "Come along, Falkenheimer, we're taking a little trip." He plunged out through the office door, shouting over his shoulder at the secretarial staff, "Back in an hour."

Bewildered, I followed him meekly out the door, along the corridor, down the short flight of stairs to the basement boiler room where Sowerby, the janitor, mixed his noxious gases, and out the boiler room door to the parking lot. Once there, we climbed into Big Bird's car—at least I assumed it was his car, though a more dilapidated relic of Detroit's art I'd never ridden in. It looked about fifty years old and had probably never been washed.

I was beginning to think my life was over. When I tried to guess where we were going the only place I could think of was a detention centre. Big Bird shouted over the noise of the engine as the car lurched out of the parking lot. "Shock therapy! That's what we need, Falkenheimer!"

I was just about to agree with him and ask him if he'd thought of having his suspension system replaced when he shouted above the noise again.

"You're just about due for some shock therapy. I've talked to Mr. Frost and I've talked to your teachers and we agree that it's time for you to start growing up."

The calm expression on his face really had me worried. I could picture myself in one of those bad TV movies where some innocent kid gets dumped in a home for delinquents and ends up turning into a teenage junkie or alcoholic or being beaten up by his fellow inmates. I couldn't stand the suspense anymore.

"Where are we going?"

"You'll see, my boy. You'll see."

We drove in silence until we reached the entrance to the university. Big Bird turned in, parked his car outside the Education Building and led the way to a small office in the north wing. I followed at his heels like an obedient puppy. He certainly knew where he was going. I wondered how many times he'd made the trip.

"Would you please tell Dr. Timmins that Mr. Bird is here to see her?" Big Bird asked a student receptionist, a pretty young woman with huge glasses.

"Dr. Timmins is expecting you. Right now she's preparing a lab class, but if you'd like to go in and wait she'll be with you in a few minutes."

So that was it! Instead of having me stabbed by sixteen-year-old hoods, Bird was going to bore me to death with more IQ tests. I didn't know which was worse.

Dr. Timmins turned out to be a short, plump woman of indeterminate age with dark hair pulled back into a messy bun. She was wearing a white medical jacket that looked as dishevelled as her hair.

A few minutes after we sat down at the back of her class the students filed out and she strode briskly over to us, hands outstretched.

"Ah, Carl, so good to see you." Her face beamed with pleasure.

I turned to look at Big Bird. He was smiling broadly at Dr. Timmins. I didn't even know he could smile! He took her hands in his with a flourish and kissed them the way they do in foreign movies.

"Ah, Catherine," he purred. "A pleasure to see you again."

"And this young man?" Dr. Timmins turned to me with a smile. I still didn't know whether the smile was phony or not, but it was better than I'd expected from a mad IQ tester.

"This is Albert Falkenheimer. I wanted you to meet him because he's almost an electrical genius. He can run any piece of electronic equipment put in his path."

"Aha, Carl, you clever man—you mean the tape recorders!"

"Precisely. I know you rely heavily on tape machines and other audio-visual equipment in the clinic, and I also know how often you have problems with maintenance, servicing and repairs. Falkenheimer here is your passport to electronic precision."

"Carl, how kind of you." Her eyes twinkled. She turned to me and pointed to the mass of equipment scattered all over the room. "Do you think you could keep it all under control, Albert?"

I swallowed a lump in my throat and nodded hastily. Was I dreaming?

"Then I think you've got yourself a part-time job. If you want it, that is."

"I want it," I heard myself saying. "Thanks a lot."

"Could you come three afternoons a week? Say from four to six?"

I nodded again. This was too good to be true—a part-time job! Would there be enough money in it to start saving up for a car? Not a new one, of course, but I had my eye on an old, beat-up 1955 Chevy that I knew I could fix up like new. Wouldn't that be something! Was this really what Big Bird had brought me here for? To fix me up with a part-time job? It didn't make sense.

"Now, Catherine, would you be so kind as to show us around the clinic? I think Albert should learn something about his new place of work." Big Bird and Dr. Timmins stood looking at one another for a brief moment. Something seemed to pass between them.

"Of course. Come this way."

The tour of the clinic was an eye-opener. We looked in on about fifteen small, egg-carton-shaped rooms where little kids of all shapes and sizes were being helped with their reading and writing by Dr. Timmins' graduate students.

"Are these kids retarded?" I asked the doctor.

"No, they're not retarded, Albert. Watch them carefully."

I watched and listened. Some of the nine- and ten-year-olds stumbling over their sentences reminded me of myself at their age, only their writing was even worse than mine. Some of them could hardly hold a pencil, let alone write anything. My own problems seemed tiny compared to the problems these kids had.

I stopped to show one of Dr. Timmins' students how to use his tape recorder in a less obtrusive way so as not to distract the little kid he was tutoring. Dr. Timmins and Big Bird stood back and watched me. What a set-up! This had obviously been planned well in advance, but I was too happy to care.

Throughout the tour of the clinic Big Bird kept asking Dr. Timmins questions about the kids and the methods of instruction. Dr. Timmins answered him but I knew most of what she said was for my benefit.

I started to ask a few questions of my own. "If these kids aren't retarded, then what's the matter with them?"

"They just have different kinds of learning handicaps that prevent them from reading and writing accurately," said Dr. Timmins.

"You mean like dyslexia?"

"Yes, that's one word used to describe their problems. But each child is different and we have to figure out the best possible approach on an individual basis."

"How come so many of the kids are boys?"

"We don't know why, but out of every five learning-handicapped children four are boys."

"Will they eventually learn to read and write?"

"Most will learn to cope in some way. A lot depends on the severity of the handicap as well as the child's level of intelligence."

I thought Dr. Timmins was putting me on. "You mean some of them are intelligent?"

"Of course!" Dr. Timmins' eyebrows arched in astonishment. "Many are extremely intelligent, Albert. Oh, years ago people thought children who couldn't write properly or who never learned to read were all retarded, but nowadays we know better. Did you know that Leonardo da Vinci, a genius, wrote a reverse script all his life? Other possible dyslexics are Albert Einstein—"

"Einstein! You're kidding!"

"Not at all. Then there's Thomas Edison, President Woodrow Wilson, Nelson Rockefeller . . . "

I didn't hear any more. My mind was reeling. My parents, my teachers and a lot of other people had tried to reassure me in the past, but I'd never believed any of them. I thought they were just being sorry for me. All those years of kids laughing and jeering at me, making fun of me when I had to read out loud in class, making remarks about my writing. Calling me a retard. He's lazy! He's slow! He's stupid! A retard!

But maybe the school counsellors and my parents had been telling me the truth. I felt like taking Dr. Timmins by the shoulders and giving her a big kiss right on her plump pink cheeks. Then I realized that Big Bird and Dr. Timmins were watching me quietly and I remembered that I should be mad about the coy way they'd set me up. Even guidance counsellors with the best intentions somehow manage to be patronizing. But this really seemed different.

"Well," Big Bird broke the silence, "we must be getting back, Catherine. Thank you for the fascinating tour. Come along, Albert."

Dr. Timmins smiled graciously. "I hope you'll enjoy working here, Albert. Please try to come tomorrow. We need your healing hands as soon as possible."

On the drive back to Carleton Big Bird didn't say a word. He just whistled tunelessly in time with the unreliable thrum of his car engine, letting the effect of everything I'd seen and heard sink in. He knew exactly what he was doing when he took me to meet Dr. Timmins. Who would have thought it? Maybe Frost was in on it too. And I had both of them figured for a pair of unfeeling dictators.

Corny though it may sound, that day really changed things for me. The more I worked at the clinic, the more I got to like and respect Dr. Timmins. I also liked the way she worked with the kids, and that made me more interested in my own work. And to think I owed it all to Big Bird.

10.

I had been looking forward to the grade-ten graduation party for a long time, but now that it was happening I didn't feel anything. It hadn't been the party itself I'd been longing for so much as a kind of landmark that pointed my way to freedom.

The party was in full swing at Bear Creek Park when I found Trivia and Doris and sat down beside them under a big chestnut tree. I'd been looking for Cathy but hadn't been able to find her. I sat hearing their voices but not their words. I was busy trying to recapture some of the feeling of excitement and anticipation I'd felt a few months earlier whenever I thought about graduation.

Trivia and Doris started arguing about something and gradually their words came through to me. It was one of those heavy conversations about the future and the quality of life and stuff like that. But I was too preoccupied with my own problems to think about the rest of the world, so I went back to my own thoughts.

With my back against the trunk of the tree, I let my gaze wander about the park. As I watched all the other kids talking and laughing my thoughts turned to Frost and Big Bird and Dr. Timmins and the little kids at the clinic. In less than a week they'd made me see things differently, as if my life were suddenly in sharp focus after being slightly fuzzy all those years.

The late afternoon breeze grew stronger and shook the heavy leaves of the chestnut tree. Under an increasingly threatening sky the grads were enjoying their last official function as Carleton students. An outdoor barbecue smoked with the dripping fat of hot dogs and hamburgers, and the rising breeze wafted the aroma of burning meat all over the park in fitful gusts. The shouts and laughter of ball players competed with the beat of music blaring from the small community hall over at the edge of the park.

As the afternoon gave way to a cooler, cloudier evening, kids began moving towards the community hall for the big grad dance. Two guys walked by wearing boots with high heels. Behind them walked two self-conscious girls in light summer dresses. I'd never seen them in anything but jeans before.

A lot of the teachers had visited the party, stayed an hour and left. But Mr. Bird and his wife were still standing over by the soft drink supply talking with Mr. and Mrs. Frost. Mrs.

Powell was sitting on the top of a picnic table surrounded by a small group of her music students. Her hand, brandishing a bottle of pop like a conductor's baton, punctuated the air around her head.

Most of the kids had come over to the park in chartered buses straight from school, but some had come on their own steam. Cathy drove over with Henry Schlieff in his dad's new Chev. I came over with Trivia on the back of his motorcycle.

I looked around for Cathy again but couldn't see her anywhere. She must have gone into the dance with Henry. Lucio and Louise Potter had been over in the thicker stands of trees earlier, smoking a joint, but now I couldn't see them either.

The party looked as if it would drag on forever and I was feeling more and more out of it. Trivia interrupted my stupor long enough to lead me over to the dance, but since neither of us was good at dancing we just hung around the door. Darkness fell and it began to rain.

By this time I'd had enough. I asked Trivia if he'd mind leaving early and after taking one look at me he said no. We headed out to the parking lot to find his motorcycle, but just as we were fastening our jackets and helmets a small knot of kids came around the back of the dance hall and passed us.

"Hey, Falko, there's Cathy," whispered Trivia.

"Who's she with?"

"Henry. And it looks like Lucio and Louise. They're leaving too."

116

We watched them walk towards Henry's car.

"Looks like Henry's been drinking," muttered Trivia. Henry looked a little unsteady and Lucio didn't look much better. They were shouting and laughing at each other like doped-up jerks.

"Come on, Triv, let's follow them!"

We jumped on Trivia's bike and started it up. I could see the group more clearly now out in the parking area. Henry opened the Chev door on the driver's side and Lucio got in beside him. Cathy got in the back behind Henry. Louise was giggling away to herself as usual.

We followed them out of the park with our headlight off until we hit the highway. The Chev headed downtown and we kept a safe distance behind it. The rain was now falling in a steady drizzle.

Half an hour later we were speeding north along Granville Street a block behind the Chev. I peered over Trivia's shoulder, through the rain, at the speedometer. We were pushing a hundred just to keep up with them. I thought of the rain on the greasy summer pavement and hoped that Trivia knew what he was doing. Cathy must be crazy to ride with those idiots, especially when they'd been drinking. I was mad at her. What gave her the idea she could change Henry? And how was risking her life going to help him?

Now Henry was driving even faster. The Chev kept switching lanes, weaving through the slower traffic. Where are the police when you want them? Trivia was having trouble keeping the speeding Chev in sight. The rain had soaked through my light jacket and my jeans were dripping. I'd been gripping the sides of the bike so tightly with my legs that there was no feeling left in my knees and thighs.

Up ahead, approaching 49th Avenue, the Chev wandered over into the curb lane just as the light changed to red. But the car didn't even slow down—just barrelled on through.

I couldn't bear to look until the sound of screeching brakes made me jerk my head up in time to see the back end of the Chev swing over to the sidewalk. It recovered, swerved to miss a car coming out of the intersection, skidded around it and crashed into a lamp standard.

I couldn't believe my eyes—the yellow overhead lights, the rain, the Chev wrapped around a pole. From what seemed far away I heard the sound of shattering glass and crunching metal.

Trivia stopped at the light and then cut through the now stationary traffic towards the wreck. I leapt from the back of the bike and rushed over to the Chev. Already a few people had gathered around the still, silent car. I pushed my way through them and the first thing I saw was Cathy's guitar smashed to pieces against the broken rear window.

Police sirens began to howl. I pulled frantically at the rear door but it was jammed. I ran around to the other side of the car—Cathy's side—jerked the door open and caught her limp body as it fell sideways into my arms. There were splatters of blood on her face and hair. I laid her down gently on the wet pavement under the yellow lights and the thin blanket of Vancouver rain.

* * *

The rain kept tapping indifferently against the window of the Emergency waiting room as I slumped in a red plastic chair, legs outstretched, staring at the toes of my soaked running shoes. The sound of the rain only accentuated the silence.

I glanced across the room at Trivia who was sitting grimly, head bent, intent, shooting owlish glances at the worried faces of Mr. and Mrs. Robinson. Nobody had spoken a word for an hour—not since the doctor had come in and told the Robinsons that Cathy had a concussion. She hadn't regained consciousness since the crash.

Henry, meanwhile, had been released after treatment for cuts and bruises—not even a broken bone! He was lucky I hadn't seen him before he left.

I didn't know about Lucio and Louise. Their parents were still inside with the doctors. Both of them had been barely conscious on arrival at the hospital. Some broken bones probably. They had been sitting on the side of the Chev that struck the pole. The blood on Cathy's face and hair had come mostly from Louise's face, which had been badly cut by shards of broken windshield glass.

The ward doors swung open. The doctor strode through them and made his way over to the Robinsons, a tired smile on his face.

"Cathy has recovered consciousness. She's going to be all right."

Mrs. Robinson said nothing but tears of relief welled up in her eyes and she began to cry quietly. Mr. Robinson smiled thankfully and put an arm around his wife's shoulders.

"May we see her, Doctor?"

The doctor hesitated. "Well, just for a minute. She shouldn't be disturbed."

I got up and signalled Trivia and we walked out into the rain together.

* * *

The next day, Friday, was our last day at Carleton High. The whole school was bubbling with holiday atmosphere—the knowledge that summer was about to begin had put a smile on every face I saw in the corridors and classrooms.

But I kept thinking about Cathy and the crash, about Henry and Lucio and Louise. The hysterical laughter during textbook check-in left me untouched. Sure, I felt a huge relief that, for me, school was finished, period! But I felt no joy in it. A gruelling wait-out had ended and now I was through with it all. What followed next, I didn't know. And somewhere at the back of my mind was the nagging worry that my real decision had yet to be made.

Some of the kids were still getting their Annuals signed. Big John Whitelaw handed me his without a word and I signed my name, *Falko Falkenheimer—All the best,* and handed it back, hoping I hadn't made too many mistakes.

In the afternoon Mr. Frost made his "Farewell to the Grads" speech, the band played *God Save the Queen* and *O Canada* and it was all over.

I collected Trivia and Doris and we headed straight for the hospital. Henry Schlieff had beaten us to it and was sitting beside Cathy's bed as we walked in. Cathy's brown eyes welcomed us with a smile.

"Well, I guess that's all I wanted to say, Cathy," Schlieff mumbled. He took Cathy's white hand and held it gingerly. But as he turned to leave Doris stopped him with a hand on his arm.

"Don't go, Henry." She shot a pleading look at Trivia.

"There's room for us all if Cathy doesn't mind," said Trivia dutifully.

Before Cathy could say anything Henry burst out, "I just came to tell Cathy something." He hesitated and blushed. "To apologize, that's all."

Her hand still on Henry's arm, Doris asked, "Have you heard how Lucio and Louise are?"

"Yeah," Henry shrugged with embarrassment. "The news isn't too good. Lucio's going to be okay, but Louise—Well, it looks like she'll need plastic surgery done on her face when the wounds heal. Her head is covered in bandages."

"We should go see her." Doris was all sympathy. "Why don't you take me over there, Henry? We'll leave poor Cathy with these two jerks. And we could look in on Lucio too."

"Sure, Doris." Henry seemed pleased with Doris's suggestion. He moved towards the door, Doris following him.

"Wait for me!" called Trivia. "I'll come with you. Check back with you later, Cathy."

I had Cathy to myself and I silently thanked Doris for having a heart of gold.

"Falko, I've been thinking about you. I'm glad you came." Cathy moved slightly and motioned me to sit on the edge of the bed.

I took her hand, at a loss for words. I felt so glad she was alive and I wanted to yell and shout and hug her, but I could still see the smashed guitar and the fragile bodies lying crumpled in the eggshell universe of a car interior.

"You sure scared everybody, Cathy," was all I managed to mumble.

"Falko, I'm sorry. What can I say? I've been a complete fool, I know." She stared at our joined hands and then placed her free hand over them. "Poor Henry. He's really upset."

I couldn't help bursting out, *"Henry's* upset? What about you? Do you realize you could have been killed? Don't tell me you still *like* the guy!"

The suspense was killing me.

"N-no. I guess I don't." Cathy looked a bit surprised by her own words. Then a smile spread across her face. "I mean, I *really* don't! You don't know how good it feels to be able to say that."

"Poor Cathy. Always trying to make people better than they are. Don't get me wrong. It's one of the things I like most about you. But there's a limit to how much you can do."

122

"Oh, yeah? I think I did a pretty good job on you, Falko." She smiled again. "Even if you *do* have a long way to go. But Henry—well, you were right. Maybe I was infatuated with everything he had going for him. Or maybe I was trying too hard to be a saint, thinking I could just talk him into changing overnight—"

"That's more like it, Cathy. I tried to tell you more than once, but you know what happened the last time we were completely honest with each other."

"You *did* tell me, Falko. It was hard to admit to myself, but you were right. I always bend over backwards to see the best in people, to avoid confronting them. Who knows? Maybe that's just my own insecurity, my own way of making people like me. You've got the opposite problem. You see more of the bad in people. So," she finished, "now you know why we fit together so well."

We sat there for what seemed a long time without saying anything. At last Cathy stirred and smiled the way she used to.

"Let's not talk about Henry or the accident. What about you, Falko? How do you feel—your last day of school?"

I shrugged. "I'm out of the cage. I'm glad it's over."

Cathy frowned and bit her lower lip. "Falko," she hesitated. "Have you ever considered that you might have built your own cage?"

"What do you mean?"

She hesitated again as she searched for words.

"Well, Carleton was never a cage for me. I've learned things there. And most of all, I've enjoyed it. If it's been a cage for you maybe that's because you weren't ready to give it a chance. Just because you've got problems reading and writing you don't have to condemn the whole system. And just because there are Harrads and Powells it doesn't have to be the end of the world."

"I don't know, Cathy, I really don't know. Even if you're right, it doesn't matter now. It's over for me. I don't want to go back to school. I want time on my own to think. I've been learning to type and I think all those hand exercises at the Learning Assistance Centre are helping me. Maybe I'll be a writer." I laughed. "Wouldn't that be ironic? One of those tortured souls with the weight of the world on his shoulders, scribbling away in a cold, lonely garret and eating dog food."

"What'll you write about?"

"Oh—you, me, the basic injustices of life. Like a memoir—*I Was a High School Reject*. How does that sound?"

"Falko, you're incurable," Cathy giggled.

In the silence that followed I ran my finger over her hand. "I'm glad you're alive, Cathy." I kissed her gently.

She smiled. "I'm glad I'm alive too, Falko."

"And—I want things to be better for both of us."

She nodded. "Me too."

124

I released her hand and stood up. "I'd better look in on Lucio and Louise, but I'll be back. How long are they going to keep you here?"

"Only another day or so. It's just bruises and a couple of cuts, but they want to make sure I'm A-1." Then she said in a quiet voice, "Thanks for coming."

Before I left I put a small parcel and envelope on the bedside table. Just a little nothing-present and a get-well card with a message. I was very careful writing the message, trying to get the spelling right for a change. I tried to express a feeling I found hard to say to Cathy to her face. I hoped she'd understand.

Later, as I left the hospital with Doris and Trivia, bright sunlight was drying the wet pavement.

11.

This morning Cathy and I jumped on a bus headed for Stanley Park. We both had something to celebrate. Yesterday she had twenty-three stitches removed from her arm and I got my first full-time summer job.

Staring out the window, I thought about a lot of stuff. School, for one thing. No more Harrad! No more Carleton High! Eleven years in the public school system were over and now I was on the threshold of something else. Whether the something else would turn out to be the freedom I'd wanted for so long or just another prison was all up to me. But at least the choice was mine to make.

I also thought about Cathy, sitting beside me lost in her own thoughts—the crash, fate, luck. Maybe there's nothing we can do about what's already laid out for us. Maybe freedom itself is just an illusion.

I used to have this recurring dream where I

was locked in a safe immersed in deep water. My hands were tied and I was holding my breath. All I had to do was get my hands free and then I could open the safe and swim to the surface. But I never managed to free them, no matter how much I struggled. Just when my lungs felt as if they were about to explode I would wake up in a cold sweat.

The weird thing about this dream was that I *knew* it was a dream even as I was drowning. So why couldn't I control the dream so that it had a happy ending? Maybe freedom is just a state of mind.

As we got off the bus at the Stanley Park stop my mind turned to brighter thoughts. Folded neatly in my wallet was my first pay cheque for two weeks of part-time work at the clinic. Yesterday, after handing me the cheque, Dr. Timmins sat me down and told me she was really happy with the job I was doing. Would I consider working for her full-time until September?

Would I *consider* it? I couldn't believe my ears! Good pay, great experience and working with people I liked. What more could I ask for? I've been floating on clouds ever since. And I may just be able to save enough for that '55 Chevy I've got my eye on.

I smiled at Cathy as we followed the park trail around Lost Lagoon.

"Are you sure you should be getting all this exercise? What if you have a relapse or something?"

"I've never felt better. It's so good to be getting out again. And besides, walking isn't going to make my arm bleed!" Cathy took a deep, appreciative breath of air.

I started to say something but got lost. Then I finally plunged in: "Cathy, I've been thinking about what you said—about making my own cage, I mean. Maybe you're right about all that stuff. But I hated being called 'Retard' by all the other kids."

I paused to collect my thoughts. Cathy didn't say anything, just gave my hand a squeeze.

"I sort of felt like that guy Rhayader. Remember him in *The Snow Goose?* He was ugly, like a monster, so he lived like a hermit, away from everyone. That's what I wanted to do—run away from everyone." I looked at Cathy. "But you always stuck up for me. You made Carleton bearable sometimes."

Cathy blinked and turned her eyes away for a second.

"But I guess I wasn't as strong as Rhayader. I've been thinking. He didn't let it all get to him. He just carried on and did his thing."

"You're stronger than you think, Falko." Cathy turned to look at me and standing there next to her I suddenly *did* feel strong.

"Maybe," I concluded, "but I always hated myself underneath it all. I wished I could just be like everyone else—normal! Know what I mean?"

"Yes," she whispered, "I know."

"And now that I've got all that figured out, I've also figured out that you were always trying to help me see this about myself, sort of like the way you wanted to help Henry."

"We all need some kind of help, Falko—or love or friendship or understanding. Call it what you like. People can't always do it on their own. We need each other."

I took Cathy's hand again as we headed down to the sea wall. We ambled past the whale pool and the Japanese War Memorial and under Lumberman's Arch to the beach. It was still early so only a few people were there. The tide was high and lapping hard against the granite sea wall. Occasionally a wave splashed us. The salt spray felt fresh against my skin.

We walked in silence. Cathy's hair blew free. Her face glowed. It was hard to believe she'd ever been in hospital.

"I love the sea," she sighed. "Don't you?"

I nodded. We stopped and looked across the harbour.

"Charm'd magic casements, opening on the foam/Of perilous seas, in faery lands forlorn."

Cathy looked at me in amazement. "You know, Falko, I've never heard you recite poetry before. Those lines are beautiful."

"I think it's by Keats," I said, hoping that I wasn't blushing. "Now if Trivia were here he'd probably be able to give the poet, title and significance. He'd write an essay off the top of his head."

The morning mist was disappearing under the heat of the sun, walkers and cyclists becoming more numerous. We followed the path along the shore by the forest cedars and down to "our" weather-bleached log on Third Beach. Dropping to the sand, Cathy leaned against the log, face upturned, eyes closed, relaxed.

Beyond the sea wall an old popcorn vendor traded and joked with some kids. A perspiring jogger with flashing blue Nikes pitter-pattered along the pathway while a black squirrel stared at him with shiny-eyed astonishment from its hemlock cranny. And over at the water's edge a small boy, serious, preoccupied, dragged his bare feet through the warm tidal pools. The heat was beginning to rise in shimmering waves from the sand, and for some unknown reason I thought about my dream again—the one where I'm drowning. It seemed like such a stupid dream now, on a perfect day like this when everything was in its proper place—popcorn and squirrels, bare feet and shimmering sand, Cathy beside me.

I looked up into the blinding sky and saw a large bird beating its wings wildly as it rose towards the sun. Silhouetted for a second it looked black, but all its feathered edges were rimmed with the colour of yellow fire. I held my breath, and then the moment was gone. The bird floated out of sight over the giant trees behind us.

I still don't know what I'm going to do with my life or even what I'm going to do at the end of the summer. I don't know if things will ever be better between my parents and me. I don't know if I'll ever be "normal" or popular or just plain happy. But lying there on the sand beside Cathy I was content to close my eyes and let the future take care of itself. I knew at last that my struggle to escape was over—both in dreams and in life.